BILLY SILVER

Daniel J. Volpe

Copyright © 2020 Daniel J. Volpe

All rights reserved

The characters and events portrayed in this book are fictitious. Any similarity to real persons, living or dead, is coincidental and not intended by the author.

No part of this book may be reproduced, or stored in a retrieval system, or transmitted in any form or by any means, electronic, mechanical, photocopying, recording, or otherwise, without express written permission of the publisher.

ISBN-13: 979-8563414983

Cover design by: Mr. Michael Squid

Printed in the United States of America

This is a work of fiction. Names, characters, businesses, places, events, locales, and incidents are either the products of the author's
imagination or used in a fictitious manner. Any resemblance to actual
persons, living or dead, or actual events is purely coincidental.

This is dedicated to all who've come before me and those who will come after. Your works scared the shit out of me and for that I'm eternally grateful.

A big thanks to the Master of Extreme Horror, Edward Lee. Mr. Lee, you have no idea the impact you've had on my career.

Thanks to Rich, who rode along with me through this crazy journey. Also, thanks to Lee A. Forman, who edited this book. I wrote it, but he cleaned it up. Check him out at tatteredgespress.com

INTRODUCTION

I've always been a fan of horror and the more extreme the better. This book is extreme in many ways. If you don't like savage killing, descriptive sex acts and profanity, this isn't for you. If you do like them, then please, enjoy the ride. It's going to be a rough one.

CHAPTER 1

Billy Silver angled the dull and slightly bent tip of the hypodermic needle under his scab. With a little more effort than he hoped for, the needle slid into the abused vein in the crook of his elbow. The dingy mixture of heroin and blood swept through his body, bringing with it a sense of euphoria he'd come to love. He sat on the toilet of his apartment. The piece of rubber tubing he used to get his veins to pop up, now loosened from his bicep. Billy leaned his head back, long blond hair clinging sweaty to his neck. The dope felt good, but not nearly as good as it should.

The first time Billy had shot dope it felt like his entire body was having one massive orgasm. The better the heroin, the better the feeling. Lately, the dope he'd been getting was weaker and weaker. The bag he just shot was weak. What should've felt like his entire body blowing a load, felt more like taking a long piss after too many beers. Still felt good, but not quite what he was looking for.

The narcotic surging through his veins, lit up his senses. When the pleasure stopped at that 'good piss' threshold, he knew the dope was weak. He pulled the needle from his arm and grabbed the old travel shave bag. The bag was his father's; Billy had taken it on his flight from his parent's house. For the last year or so, the bag was his rig. In junkie speak, it was where he kept the tools of the trade for one such as himself. In it were a few hypos, the rubber tubing, a couple of plastic bottle caps, a bent spoon (also stolen from his parent's house), a plastic lighter with a marihuana leaf on it and half a dozen empty wax paper envelopes that once held tiny amounts of heroin.

Billy got his rig packed up and stood on wobbly legs. He was thin and shirtless. His blond hair, which was once golden, now more resembled hay animals spent days shitting and pissing on. In a vain attempt to cover the scar on his cheek, Billy grew a weak, wispy beard and mustache. He knew it looked like shit, but at this stage in the game, he really didn't give a fuck.

Billy lifted the toilet seat, taking aim at his favorite stain in the bowl. He noticed a dark ring around the base of his cock. He touched it and smelled his fingers; shit, shit and blood. He smiled at the revolting odor. Jeannie must've wanted a good fuck in the ass last night and clearly, he'd obliged her. Piss came out at every which angle, some on the bowl, some of the floor. He left without flushing.

The rest of his studio apartment was no better. The kitchen consisted of a hot plate and coffee pot. He stumbled toward the latter.

Jeannie, his sort of girlfriend, was passed out, face down, on the black futon. She wore only a white pair of underwear, which had seen better days. Her bleach blond hair covered her face. A thick stripe of her natural brown hair contrasted in the middle of her head. Billy thought she looked like a reverse skunk. She let out a long, wet fart, mumbled and turned.

Well, now you smell like one too, you nasty bitch, he thought.

One of her breasts peaked out from underneath her. She was only 27, but years of drinking, drugging and smoking had taken its toll on her. Rather than look like a nice, firm handful, her tit looked more like an orange that fell behind the fridge and rotted. She mumbled again, brushing hair from her face.

Billy saw the damage. The left side of her face was discolored and swollen; some dried blood rested at the corner of her mouth. He looked at his right hand and saw the cuts on his knuckles. He didn't remember hitting her, but he was sure it was for a good reason. That reason could've been anything, but probably had something to do with booze or drugs. It usually was, but sometimes it was just Billy's great temper.

Luckily, her gas had stopped. After a good ass-fuck, Jeannie would be letting them rip. Hopefully she'd gotten them all out overnight.

Billy looked on the counter at the tin coffee can. He knew it was empty when he picked it up.

"Motherfucker," he whispered, setting it back down. He should've thrown it out because he knew tomorrow he'd do the same song and dance, just like he did yesterday. He opened the top of the coffee machine and saw old grinds. He filled the pot with water and dumped it into the machine. Something that vaguely resembled coffee began to drip out.

Billy grabbed a cigarette and sat at the small table. It overflowed with garbage, mostly half rot-ten take-out containers and pizza boxes. He found an ashtray that looked like a forest of butts and dumped it into one of the pizza boxes. A cloud of ash rose up and he closed it, putting the ashtray in front of him. His head, which he'd rested in his left hand, was throbbing. Too much alcohol and not enough dope. He pulled on the cigarette, his eyes closed. A curl of ash fell on the table, missing the ashtray. Something buzzed and he peeled his eyes open.

At first, he thought it was Jeannie doing herself with her little rabbit (she always kept it nearby in the event Billy couldn't get it up), but another ass trumpet from her signaled she was still out cold.

It was his cell phone, which he must've put on vibrate the night before.

"Fuck," Billy looked outside, realizing how sunny it was. It had to be close to noon and he had band practice.

Billy and 3 other guys made up the Hudson Valley's premier metal band, *Shit Fist*. It started in the garage of one of his friend's houses when they were in high school. Since then they had grown into a mildly successful band. They weren't going on tour anytime soon, but they got paid to play shows. Usually it was only a local venue, but hey, it was something.

He put the cigarette in his mouth and began tossing shit off the table to find his phone. The cracked screen showed a little vibrating alarm clock and almost dead battery. Billy breathed a sigh of relief when he saw he'd set an alarm for 11 AM. Very responsible of him.

Even though Billy was lead guitar and vocals, he'd almost been thrown out of the band numerous times. He knew the other guys had interviewed people for his spot and *Shit Fist* was the only good thing in his life. No more fuck ups.

Billy stubbed out his cigarette in the ashtray, the first tree in the new forest. The piss water, he called coffee, was done. He grabbed the least disgusting mug and filled it up. The first sip burned his lips, but the heroin dulled the pain. It tasted like shit; no amount of dope could help that.

He lit up another cigarette, evaluating what he had left in the pack. Billy set the cup down and put his smoke in the ashtray. He then grabbed his pride and joy, his guitar.

Nestled in a hard case lined with the softest of velvet sat his 2004 Gibson Les Paul. It was the smoothest color of frost blue with an ebony fretboard (a limited run, which he'd tell anyone who would listen). He lifted it from the case and walked over to the small amp. He plugged the guitar in, a little whine of feedback shrieked. Billy sat, took a drag on his cigarette and began checking his tune.

"What the actual fuck?" moaned Jeannie, sitting up on the futon. Her hair was sweat- slicked to her forehead. She put a hand to her throbbing face, feeling the swollen lumps on her cheek. Her hand recoiled, as if she'd touched something hot. "Jesus Christ, Billy," she said, slightly slurring thanks to the fat lip.

Billy, ignoring her, tuned his guitar through a veil of cigarette smoke. He plucked at the strings with his favorite guitar pick, which had a tasteful and rather hairy vagina on it. Above it was written, 'good bush' and on the back was a picture of President Bush (the second one) with a line through his face and said, 'bad bush'. He laid the cigarette in the ashtray and watched Jeannie walk over.

Her small, yet somehow saggy tits swayed as she navigated the room. She still held her head, her fingers lost in the rat's nest of her hair. Without asking she grabbed his cigarette and took a deep drag.

Jeannie went to put the cigarette back in the ashtray, but missed.

"What the fuck," said Billy, picking it up as it left a neat burn on the table.

She ignored him, making her way to the coffee pot. She poured a cup and sat down.

Billy knew he didn't look much better, but she looked like microwaved shit.

Her skin, which had been porcelain-like as a kid, was dry and veiny. Her face, like Billy's, showed the losing battle with teenage acne. She even had a few fresh ones popping up.

"I need a smoke," she said, taking his pack. There were only 4 left after she took one. "And a bag." She was referring to a bag of heroin. The last one either of them had was currently in Billy's bloodstream.

Billy grabbed his smoke back, looking at Jeannie. He had an idea. Always the trickster, Billy Silver, always the trickster.

"Well, there's only one bag left," he lied, setting his guitar gently on the floor.

Jeannie perked up. "Let's split it. I really need a little to take the edge off." She wasn't detoxing yet, but she could feel it in the back of her mind. It was her little hitchhiker that never seemed to get off. "Plus, my face is killing me." She absently rubbed her damaged face, wincing as she pushed too hard.

"Yeah, my bad. Must've had too much Jack

last night." He knew that was a lie. He probably had too much, but truthfully he liked punching her. It didn't take too much for him to use the excuse. He gave her a little grin, hoping to smooth it over, especially if he wanted what he was going to ask for. "Nah, we can't split it. T-Rex has been getting weak shit lately. That bag will barely get you high, let alone both of us." Billy grinned at her. "I will let you have it, but..." He trailed off.

"But what?" She asked, adding her cigarette butt to the forest.

"I could really use a blowjob before band practice," he said. Already his cock was stiffening at the thought. Billy wasn't blessed with many things in life, but his member was one of the few. He weighed maybe 155, but was 5 pounds of dick.

"Really?" She whined. "Billy, my head is killing me and the last thing I want to do is to move it back and forth. Can't we just fuck real fast?" Jeannie was almost a pro at sucking cock. The things she could do with that filthy mouth were downright divine. The only problem was she hated the taste of cum. Couldn't stand it. This wasn't an issue for Billy; as long as it came out of him he didn't care where it went. He'd obliged her by shooting his spunk on her saddlebags or face, but not her mouth.

"I don't want that beat pussy," he grinned, "kidding, kidding," he put his hands up when she scowled. It was true though. Her pussy looked like a punched lasagna covered in hair. He'd fuck her, sure, but if he could get her asshole or mouth, he'd take them first. God forbid he accidently knocked her up. She had an IUD, at Billy's insistence. He didn't feel like paying for another abortion.

"Plus, I know you didn't shower yet and you fucked me in the ass last night." It was as if her ass reminded her and she wiggled in her chair. She could still feel his load inside her.

Billy checked his phone. "I have to leave in a few minutes, so make up your mind." He was rubbing himself through his shorts. "No sucky, no dopey," he told her.

She rubbed at her arms. There was no way she'd make it through the day without getting high. "Fine, make it fast."

"Atta girl," Billy said, dropping his shorts. He walked over to the futon, dick bobbing up and down. There was a fine crust of shitty blood under his helmet. He sat on the edge of the futon.

Jeannie put her hair in a loose ponytail and assumed the position. "Jesus, Billy, your cock smells terrible," she said.

Honestly, Billy couldn't remember if he'd showered the day before. He was sure he had a pungent aroma of ball sweat and feces.

"It would smell worse if I fucked that box of yours. Now, get sucking or I'm shooting that bag and leaving."

She retched once and got to work.

Every time she blew him, he was in awe of her skill. Her ball play was what put her over the top for him. A solid 10 out of 10 in cocksucking. Billy lay as still as possible, knowing if he started squirming or moaning she'd know he was about to blow. Then, he passed that magical threshold. He looked down at her going to town. The corners of her mouth were tinted brown.

Here it comes, you fucking bitch, he thought, grabbing the back of her head. He thrust his cock down her throat and erupted.

Jeannie, gagging from the meat missile in her throat and the gout of semen, began to retch.

Billy let her go just as she started puking.

A torrent of vomit, a mixture of Ramen noodles and cum, spewed from her, splashing on the floor.

"You fucking asshole!" she yelled, a noodle stuck to her chin. She wiped her mouth with the back of her hand.

Billy swung, open handed this time; he felt generous, and smacked her right in the face.

Her already swollen face flared to life in pain. Fresh blood dribbled from her mouth.

"You're fucking lucky," he said, pulling his shorts back on. "I should've punched you, you fucking skank."

Jeannie sat on the floor, the pool of vomit running towards her, a look of confusion on her face.

"You shot the last bag last night," he lied. "We said we were going to split it, but you got too fucked up and took it." He rooted around for a pair of pants. "I have some empties in my rig. Suck on them and maybe you won't detox too hard." He finished dressing and put his guitar in the case. "We'll go see T-Rex later and get a bundle." Billy looked around and grabbed his smokes off the table, along with his phone. "Clean this shit up. I'll be back later."

Billy walked out.

Jeannie sat on the floor. She slowly got to her feet and spat. She hoped the toothpaste could get rid of the taste of cum, shit and puke, but she doubted it.

CHAPTER 2

Billy walked down the sidewalk, guitar case in his hand. It was a beautiful fall day, well it would've been if he hadn't been in this shithole city.

Instead of crisp fresh air, the breeze carried the odor of old urine and beer wafting from the alleys. Dead leaves mixed with cigarette wrappers and empty bags of heroin, blew around as if they belonged together. Small piles of refuse gathered in abandoned doorways.

Billy had lived in Newburgh for almost 5 years. After being so kindly kicked out of his parent's house in the Town of Woodbury, he decided for a change of scenery.

Newburgh was a picturesque city; a long, wide main street, old rows of brownstone houses and of course, the Hudson river. From afar it looked great. Until you got up close and saw it for the mess it was. Your chances of being a victim of a violent crime were quite high and Billy was one of those stats.

Shortly after he'd moved to Newburgh, he was walking to one of the many bodegas to buy some smokes. A group of 5 teenagers beat the shit out of him for a lousy ten bucks. Luckily, they didn't do any serious damage, but he was banged up pretty good. Life had gotten better for him after that, which he was thankful for. He had nowhere else to go, so he had to make do. Once the locals started seeing him around, they realized he was one of them, which was good. His white ass stood out like a sore thumb in a city that was 90% black or Hispanic. Billy didn't mind living there, actually he kind of liked it. There was no fake shit, like in the prissy area he'd grown up in. Either people didn't like you and kicked your ass, or they did and just ignored you. Many of the Hispanic families were illegals, so they didn't want any trouble. He still had the seeds of racism sown from years of living with his parents, but they hadn't grown much. Almost all of the black people he saw were decent, hard-working folks. Some of them, like his dealer, T-Rex, were not.

Billy enjoyed heroin, but he loved alcohol. He

always told people he drank like a homeless person; whatever, whenever. If he had a choice it was beer and a lot of it. His metabolism and lack of any nutritional food kept him from getting the classic beer belly.

He walked into A and S convenience store under the sound of bells and the eyes of many cameras. Billy looked at the beer cooler and grabbed 2 tall boys of Rolling Rock, his favorite.

He set it on the counter. "This and a pack of Camels," he said to the clerk, an Indian looking gentleman. Billy opened his wallet and saw $10 and $20. He grabbed the $20 and folded it up. It was the last of the counterfeit money he'd bought from Dicky.

Richard "Dicky" Lyboldt, was a jack of all trades. If you needed something stolen, something broken or if you had to get rid of stolen shit, Dicky was your man. Recently, through one of his many seedy connections, Dicky had come across almost a thousand dollars in fake money. Now, it wasn't perfect, but it was mostly small bills, which people never checked. He sold them for $.50 on the dollar, a real bargain.

Billy had bought $100 worth of the fake money and was down to his last $20.

The clerk rang him up, keeping his eye on a few shady looking kids, who'd just walked in. He barely glanced at the money when Billy handed it over. He gave Billy back five singles and a handful of change.

"Thanks," said Billy, taking the bag from him.

Once outside he cracked open his first beer. He walked down the street, with time to spare. For once he wouldn't be late. He might have a little buzz drinking 2 tall boys on an empty stomach, but he'd be on time.

Billy finished his first beer and tossed the can on the sidewalk. It wasn't littering to him, some bum would come grab it and get a $.05 deposit on it. Whatever he could do to help the less fortunate.

One of the many vacant storefronts wasn't so vacant anymore, Billy noticed.

"Get tattooed, get paid," Billy read the sign out front of the store. A short stocky guy swept the sidewalk in front of the business.

The man with the broom had on blue jeans and a tight flannel shirt. The sleeves were rolled up, revealing well muscled and heavily tattooed forearms. He was bald and Billy could see a thick mustache. Billy thought he looked like an old-school strongman. The guy who was on the posters in a unitard, lifting a 1-ton barbell over his head.

"New place?" Billy asked, stopping next to the guy. He took out his old pack of cigarettes and lit up. He checked the time on his phone, but it had died.

The guy stopped sweeping and looked up at Billy.

"Yeah, just getting set up," he replied, looking Billy up and down. It wasn't quite a predatory glare, like he'd seen out of some people, but more of an evaluation.

"You're paying for ink?" asked Billy, blowing smoke away from the man's face.

He leaned on the broom, "Yes, sir," he said with a grin. "Ya, interested?"

"Depends," Billy replied. "What is it and how much?"

"Nothing crazy. I have a few artists who've been out of the game for a while, but are very good. They just need a little practice before the grand opening. The tattoos are usually geometric shapes and such. That's really what they love." He pointed to his forearm at a pattern of lines that roughly formed a shark. "I'm paying a hundred for each tattoo, but only to the first 5 people. I'm not made of money," he smiled.

"Cool, thanks for the info and good luck," Billy said, tossing his cigarette in the sewer.

"Artemis," said the man, holding out his hand, "but everyone calls me Art."

Billy took it and could see something, ever so slightly, change in the man's face. It was subtle, like he'd smelled something bad, but it was there.

"Billy," he said, uneasy for a moment. More abruptly than he intended, Billy broke the handshake. "Nice to meet you, but I have to get going." He tapped the side of the guitar case. "Band practice."

Art nodded, "Sure, sure. I need to finish up here anyway. Maybe I'll see you around."

Billy was already walking away. "Sure thing," he said over his shoulder. He turned the corner and opened his last beer. A shiver ran down his spine. *I just have to piss,* he thought. Thinking of the change in Art's face, he shivered again.

* * *

Billy could hear his bandmates as he walked into the building. He was on time, for once, but they were usually early.

"Holy shitballs," said Dillon, who held one drumstick above his snare. "Is that Billy?" He checked his watch, "and on time too?"

The other two bandmates that made up *Shit Fist* jeered at him as well.

"Yeah, fucking yeah," said Billy, smiling. He chugged the other beer and had a pretty decent buzz going. Which was good, because the bag of dope was wearing off. He put his guitar case down. "Are we going to practice or what?" He asked. Billy had a second wind. He didn't know if it was the odd meeting with Art, the heroin or the beer. Either way, he felt pretty good. Felt like he wanted to rock the fuck out.

"Who are you and where the fuck is Billy?" asked Vin. He was the lone bass player. His hair was buzzed close to the scalp. Both of his earlobes were stretched to the max with heavy gauges. His spindly arms were covered in shitty tattoos.

Billy ignored them and did a level check on the mic. He lowered it an inch or two.
He opened his guitar case and plugged in. Everyone else looked at him; they were ready and waiting.

"Ok, Dillon," he said to his drummer, "tap us in."

Dillon, on cue, tapped his sticks together. "One, two, one, two, three, four."

The final rehearsal of the original *Shit Fist* was underway.

❈ ❈ ❈

Band practice ended 3 hours later. Billy's ears were ringing, but felt great. Almost like he just had a great workout, something he hadn't done in years. His only issue was the buzz had worn off. Well, he'd fix that.

Billy lit a smoke as he walked back into the tiny bodega.

"Hey, no, no, no!" Yelled the clerk.

Billy looked around in shock. *What the fuck is his problem?* He thought.

"Outside, now!" the clerk yelled.

Billy realized he couldn't smoke in the store.

"My bad," he said, tossing the smoke out of the door and onto the street. "You fucking camel jockey," he whispered, turning towards the beer cooler. He bought 3 tall boys and had the first one empty before he reached the corner. Again, he tossed the can on the ground.

He took his time getting home. For one, he wanted to finish his beers in peace. New York had open container laws, but the cops really didn't give a shit. Second, he didn't want to hear Jeannie's mouth. He knew she'd be detoxing. *Probably has the shakes right now.*

Billy let out a violent burp as he fished his keys out of his pocket. He was good and drunk now. Not blackout, oh no, but he chugged three tall boys in less than a half hour. Yup, he was feeling alright.

Just as he figured, Jeannie was feeling the pangs of her addiction.

She lay on the futon wearing a loose t-shirt and sweatpants; a wet washcloth over her eyes. After being in the fresh air, the apartment smelled like a hobo den.

Billy lit a cigarette, the first out of his new pack, just to cover the odor.

Jeannie, without pulling the washcloth from her eyes, said, "That was a long ass practice."

Billy put his guitar case away. He was hungry. Beer and a few chips were the only things he'd consumed all day.

"It wasn't any longer than usual," he responded, looking for something to eat. He realized it was almost 4 PM. The sky was starting to darken. "Besides, we have a gig tonight, so we had to fix a few things."

Jeannie hated his music. She favored hip hop and rap and had no use for the shit he called music. Normally, she'd tell him they needed to fix everything, but she needed a fix of dope and didn't want a fight.

"So, do you think we can get a few bags before the show?" She asked, removing the washcloth, propping up on one elbow.

Billy found a can of beef stew and peeled back the top. He plunged a spoon into the congealed mess. He didn't want to wait for the hot plate to warm up. The greasy meat left a film on his teeth.

"Depends," he said, swallowing a bite. His head was fuzzy from the alcohol. "How much cash do you have?"

"I have $20," she said, scratching her arms. Jeannie didn't have the track marks on her arms, like Billy. Even though she looked like a junkie in every way, shape and form, she tried to hide it. Rather than shoot up in her arms, she preferred in between the toes. She did the child's nursery rhyme of *This Little Piggy* when choosing which toes she was going to shoot between.

"Where the fuck did you get a 20 from?" Billy said, brown gravy sputtering from his mouth.

"I, ah," she stammered, "just had it saved for a rainy day," she said.

"Bullshit," Billy replied, "you probably sucked a cock for it."

She didn't answer.

"So can we go or not?" she asked impatiently.

"Can I fucking eat first?" He said, another spoonful of cold stew into his mouth.

She stood up and put her shoes and coat on.

Billy finished. He left the can on the table. "Ok," he said, "let's go see T-Rex."

❈ ❈ ❈

Terrance "T-Rex" Harrison, stood on the corner of William and South William Street. All 25 years of his life were spent in the City of Newburgh. He started selling drugs with his older brother, Slick, when he was 7 years old. The youngins, as they were called, were the best for the older dealers.

They would usually carry the drugs or sometimes guns, for the older boys. Cops would rarely check a child, and if he was caught, wouldn't get charged. When T-Rex was 14, he watched Slick get gunned down by a Hispanic gang a few blocks over. Candle and liquor bottle monuments were erected and shirts with Slick's face on them were passed out. Within a week, his baby's mother was fucking a new guy.

Life went on and the drugs continued to flow. T-Rex stepped in, taking over the family business his brother brought him into.

T-Rex stood in a black parka that was at least 2 sizes too big for him. He was short and thin, but the oversized jacket made him look huge. A pink scar creased his lip, courtesy of a box cutter wielded during a fight.

Billy saw him and his muscle man, Deet, standing on the corner. He had a sweaty fist wrapped around a 20 and 10 dollar bill.

"Yo, Rex," Billy said, from farther away, as to not startle the dealer.

T-Rex turned and saw Billy. He popped a Newport in his mouth and lit it.

"You got a lot of nerve coming back, my nigga," he said, the cigarette bobbing up and down as he spoke.

Billy looked around as if he were talking to someone else.

"Who, me?" Billy asked, a hand to his chest in shock.

Rex closed the distance, grabbing Billy by the jacket. "Yeah, motherfucker, you." Rex said. Deet, all 350 pounds of him, didn't even move. Rex didn't need help with a dopesick junkie.

"I didn't do shit," Billy said, trying to sound hard, but in reality he was about to piss himself.

Rex let him go and slapped him.

Billy wanted to fight back, but he was terrified. Plus, he needed dope.

"Chill, my dude." Billy put his hands up in a defensive stance. Something he'd seen Jeannie do many times when he'd had too much. "What's the deal?"

Rex blew smoke in his face. "You ripped me off, that's the fucking deal."

Dicky said the counterfeit money was good, but not perfect. Billy paid Rex with $60 worth of fake money last time he bought from him.

Billy still feigned ignorance. "Come on, man. That ain't me." He took one of his own cigarettes out. Jeannie stayed silent, just watching the exchange.

"I don't give a fuck if it's you or not. You gave me fake ass money. Almost got my nigga, Deet arrested." He looked to his bodyguard, "Eh yo, Deet come here a minute."

The big man waddled over. "Tell this nigga what happened with that funny money."

Deet looked like a young Uncle Phil from *The Fresh Prince of Bel Air*.

"Man, I tried registering my girl's car and the motherfucking DMV told me that money was fake. I'm on probation, motherfucker. Almost got my ass sent back to the county."

Billy looked outraged. "Motherfucker," he said. "This cocksucker ripped me too. I sold a GPS I swiped from a car to some fucking guy." He lied like it was second nature, which it was in his case. "He must've had the fake money. I'll fix his ass next time I see him." Hopefully the ruse worked. He couldn't afford to walk away empty handed. His addiction wasn't as bad as Jeannie's, but he was starting to come down and knew he needed something to get him through his show later on.

"So can we get a half a bundle or what?" Billy asked, pulling $30 from his pocket.

T-Rex grabbed the money from Billy's hand

and laughed.

"Nigga, you ain't getting shit." He pocketed the money. "You ain't getting nothing until you get me the rest of my money. This is your fucking down payment," he flicked his cigarette at Billy's feet. "You lucky I don't charge you interest. Get the fuck outta my sight."

Jeannie whimpered. She was nauseous and this was the worst thing anyone could've said.

"Rex, wait," Billy said, taking a step towards the dealer. Deet stepped in, his bulk between them.

"I told you, nigga. Get the fuck out of here before I have Deet fold you up."

"What about her?" Billy said pointing to Jeannie. "She sucks a mean dick."

Jeannie looked at the ground, but didn't speak. She had her arms across her chest, swaying just slightly. At this point she'd do almost anything for a bag of dope.

"Or fuck her. She'll even take it in the ass. Trust me, I know," he nervously grinned.

"Nigga," Rex said looking him in the eye, "let me tell you a few things about myself. First off, I don't fuck with white bitches. Get me a rich, dark Nubian queen and I'll drop a load faster than a motherfucker. Second, I don't fuck with junkies, even if they are my color preference." He looked at his hulking friend. "What about you, Deet? You want to get your dick wet?"

The big man eyed her up and down. "One bag for a blowjob," he said.

Billy said, "One bag each."

Deet nodded and headed towards the alley. "Come on, bitch. Time's money."

Jeannie looked at Billy, like she was having second thoughts and followed Deet into the alley.

She squatted down in front of his crotch. She didn't dare kneel on the dirty ground. "Do you have a rubber?" She asked.

Deet shot her a glance. "I don't use a jimmie for a blowjob." He said, unzipping his fly.

She could smell him already; grungy, an almost animal scent. "Just don't nut in my mouth," she said.

"Don't worry, baby girl. Just get to work."

Billy waited for her at the end of the block. She came back wiping her mouth with the back of her hand.

"Did he cum in your mouth?" he asked.

She nodded, spitting on the ground. "The first shot and then I pulled my head away. It tasted like old fryer grease." She shivered at the aftertaste.

Luckily she didn't have anything in her stomach or she would've puked.

"The dope?" he asked.

She looked at him and sighed. "They only gave me one bag, Billy. He said if you wanted one, you could suck his dick. Sorry."

"Motherfuckers," he said louder than he probably should have.

"Billy," she shushed him, looking around. No one heard, or if they did, they didn't care. "We'll split it." She hoped he agreed to it. He could get nasty and just take it from her.

"Whatever," he said. "Let's just get back and cook it up. Something's better than nothing. After I get paid later, I'll get a full bundle tomorrow and squash this fucking debt."

Within 10 minutes of getting home, they both had needles in their bodies. The dope was a little stronger than the last batch, but still weak. Jeannie was feeling good, staring at the ceiling, nodding off.

Billy, on the other hand, needed something else to take the edge off. He found half a bottle of vodka in the pile of takeout on the table. Two hours until Dillon was picking him up. Plenty of time to get fucked up.

* * *

Jeannie was up. She ate a cold toaster pastry, getting crumbs all over the futon.

"I don't know, Billy. What are we going to do?" She asked, absently chewing and staring at the wall.

Billy sat at the table, smoking a cigarette. Everything was hazy and spinning. He had finished the bottle of vodka an hour ago. Luckily, he scrounged together a few bucks in change and bought a few more cheap beers. Now, he was good and fucked up. An ash snake fell from his cigarette, but he was so trashed he didn't even notice.

"We don't get our welfare money for a week," she was looking at him now, but he wasn't paying attention. "I'm not going to make it for a week." She knew Billy would make some money tonight, but normally it was around $50. That was just enough to cover the debt and get a few bags, if T-Rex decided not to charge interest. They would only be able to get two bags of heroin, which would only keep them level for another day.

Billy turned his head ever so slowly towards her. There were two of her and they were swimming. She wouldn't shut the fuck up and his last nerve was frayed. He'd had too much.

Jeannie got up and walked over to the table. She took one of his cigarettes. "We need cash soon." She was looking at him, but he was still looking out into space. "Billy. Billy!" she yelled, snapping her fingers in his face.

Slowly, he turned his head towards her.

"Are you fucking listening to me? I said, we need fucking cash. We need dope. I'm going to be puking and shitting my brains out in 24 hours." She put the cigarette in her mouth. The lighter wavered as she tried to light her cigarette. Finally, she got it.

Billy checked his phone, which he'd finally charged. Dillon would be picking him up for the concert in 15 minutes or so.

"What about your guitar?" She asked. "I know you love it, but what if you pawned it? Just for a little while and then buy it back. Our government checks will be in and you can get it back." Her mind was racing, thinking about how much money they could get for it. "What about tomorrow? Do the gig tonight and pawn it tomorrow. You'll be able to get it back before your next show and-" Even though

Billy was drunk, he was still fast.

He punched her in the face. Not a huge wind-up punch, but just a quick jab. It was more than enough to break her nose.

Jeannie reached up, grabbing her face, accidently burning herself with the cigarette. Blood poured from her fingers, running down her arms.

Billy was up on wobbly legs and coming at her. His next blow, a lazy hook, hit her in the temple, knocking her out of the chair.

Jeannie was whimpering. Her nose, crooked and swollen.

Billy, even as drunk as he was, knew he needed his hands to play his guitar, so he began kicking.

"You fucking skank bitch!" he yelled, kicking her ribs. "I'd kill you before I got rid of my fucking guitar." He kicked again and tossed his cigarette into her hair.

Jeannie shrieked as her hair started to smolder. She pulled her hands from her face to put the flame out.

Billy, ever the opportunist, kicked her square in the face. She gagged when her front tooth snapped off, rocketing down her throat.

Jeannie wailed, her face a bloody mess. The exposed nerve of her tooth getting its first glimpse of light.

"Oh shit, your hair is on fire," Billy slurred, a grin on his face. "Let me help you." He pulled his cock out and unleashed a torrent of piss onto her face and head.

She raised a defensive hand, trying to block the stream.

Billy laughed and switched his aim. He felt like he was at the carnival and trying to fill up the balloon with the water gun. Her mouth was full of piss and blood. The last dribbles of piss landed on the floor, but he didn't give a fuck.

Jeannie lay in a heap. She cried through her hands, which were back over her ruined face. Her legs were pulled up tight in the fetal position, in the event Billy decided to give her a parting shot. She needed to spit the blood and piss out, but didn't want to remove her hands covering her face.

Billy's phone beeped. Dillon was downstairs. "Clean this fucking shit up. I'll be back later." He grabbed his jacket and guitar and left.

Billy opened the back door of Dillon's car and laid his guitar on the seat.

"What's up, man?" said Dillon. His nose wrinkled. "Jesus Christ, you fucking stink like a brewery."

Billy slid into the front seat. He took Dillon in with glassy eyes.

"I had a few fucking beers, so what?" Billy ran his hands through his hair. "Let's go, motherfucker."

Dillon eyed him. Billy was trashed. He put his car into gear and started driving.

"Are you gonna be good to play?" Dillon asked him. He cast a sidelong glance at Billy.

Billy lit up a cigarette. "Yeah, why the fuck wouldn't I be?" He cracked the window and watched the smoke get sucked out. "I've been way more fucked up than this. I just need a Red Bull or two and I'll be set."

"You sure?" asked Dillon, watching his friend out of the corner of his eye.

Billy stared at him. "Just fucking drive."

They arrived at the venue, *The Lucky Draw*, down at the Hudson River waterfront. It was a small venue, only able to hold a few hundred people.

Dillon drove to the back of the venue where the loading and unloading area was. Vin and Kyle were busy with the equipment in the van.

Billy stumbled out of the car and started walking towards his band mates. Dillon grabbed his arm.

"Dude, we got the loading. Just go inside and

get some water in you. Try and sober up a little. Please."

Billy looked at his friend, who was constantly moving. He thought all the booze was in his system, but he realized he was still going up the BAC scale. He nodded, shakily turning towards the front of the venue.

Maurice, the biggest, blackest bouncer in the world, stood at the door. He waved Billy in, knowing him by face.

Billy shot him a sloppy salute and walked in.

Ear-shattering music assaulted his senses. The cloying stench of hot bodies rode the waves of sound. It was a welcoming environment. Billy staggered over to the bar. Jeff was behind there, so Billy knew he was getting free drinks.

Jeff was in his mid-50s, cue ball bald, with a little pot belly. He wore a tight band t-shirt and even tighter jeans. An upside-down crucifix hung from his left ear. He was gay as the day is long and had the biggest crush on Billy. He caught a glimpse of Billy's dong in the bathroom one day, and was in love.

"Hey there, Wild Bill," Jeff said, leaning over the bar. "What can I getcha? A beer, a shot, a suck job?" He winked.

Billy was used to the faggy come ons, but he couldn't care less. As long as the drinks were free.

"I think I'll pass on the suck job, but I'll take Red Bull vodka," he slurred, smiling at his admirer.

"Damn shame." He started making the drink. "I bet with this mouth, I could turn you."

Billy thought about Jeannie's prowess with her mouth. Her blowjob days were going to be on hold for a while until her busted face healed.

Jeff handed him the drink. "That's on me. Maybe you can be too." He winked, turning to another customer.

Billy sipped his drink. It was nearly all vodka. Just how he liked it. He drank it down in three gulps. It burned in that loving way. He turned to the stage. Some shitty high school band was shrieking on stage. *Fucking trash,* he thought.

Billy swayed. The alcohol was kicking his ass and he loved it. He went back up to the bar for a refill. Jeff obliged, probably hoping to get him drunk enough to suck his dick. The band had ended their set, thank fucking God.

"Alright, Newburgh," the MC said, grabbing the microphone as the band started clearing their equipment. "Up next we have one of our local bands, *Shit Fist*." The announcement of the band brought about a mix of laughs and applause.

Billy finished his drink and ran back to the bar. He wasn't quite as drunk as he'd like to be. This was his last chance. Desperate times call for desperate measures. He flagged Jeff down. Billy moved to the side of the bar, near the bar flap.

Billy whispered in Jeff's ear. "If I let you touch my cock under the bar flap, will you fill a water bottle with vodka?" He was already unzipped; his dick hanging out of his fly.

Jeff smiled, reaching under the bar flap, grabbing Billy's flaccid penis. Even soft it was impressive. Jeff shook, giving it a small stroke before letting go.

"You're fucking killing me," he said to Billy, dumping out a water bottle and filling it with vodka.

Billy tucked his dick away and took the bottle. "Thanks," he winked at Jeff. *Keep him strung along and get free drinks. Easy peasy.*

"Nice of you to show up," said Vin, who lingered behind the stage setting up.

Billy sipped out of the water bottle. Dillon gave him a nod.

"My bad. I wasn't feeling well and had to shit." He rubbed his stomach. "All emptied out and ready to roll." He was fucked up, but Vin seemed to not notice. Or he was choosing to ignore it. Like when daddy slaps mommy at the dinner table and asks you to pass the fucking peas. You pass the fucking peas like it's the most normal thing in the world. Mommy, a hand welt bright red on her face, tears hovering on the brink of falling. She plasters a forced smile as she cuts up your meat, hoping everything is hot. She can't handle another slap.

"Well plug in and let's get our sound checks," Vin said. They did just that and shockingly, sounded great. Vin gave a thumbs up to the MC. It was showtime.

Billy cradled his guitar in one hand and chugged from the bottle of vodka. There it was. Now he'd had too much. The curtains opened and a sea of sweaty faces looked back at him.

"What's up, motherfuckers!" he yelled into the mic, his speech slurred. Some of the crowd cheered, but most just looked apprehensive. "We are the legendary *Shit Fist* and we're here to fuck your asses raw!" he growled.

Dillon started them off, tapping his sticks.

On cue, just as in rehearsal, Billy let out his first line of lyrics. Promptly followed by a stream of hot puke. He'd never projectile vomited before, until now.

Vodka and half-digested beef stew covered the front row of the crowd. Billy watched a fat girl, with Smurf-shit blue hair, get a mouthful of spew. She spat it out, but too late. Her own torrent of vomit poured from her mouth, splashing on the floor.

People panicked and screamed, trying to get away from the puddles of vomit and vomit covered concert goers.

Billy swayed on stage, watching the chaos he'd unleashed. He burped up one more bubble of puke and passed out.

CHAPTER 3

Billy felt like he'd been put through a meat grinder. He was afraid to open his eyes, for two reasons: he could feel the sun and knew it would kill his hung over eyes, plus, he wasn't sure where the fuck he was.

He felt his back against the floor and he was pretty sure it was his place. With a deep breath, he cracked his eyes open.

The sun tormented him, singeing his eyes down to the optic nerve. His mouth tasted like feral cats had a gang bang in there and then proceeded to shit everywhere. He looked around and to his relief, he was in his apartment.

Jeannie was nowhere to be seen and Billy was relieved. He didn't need to deal with her bullshit.

His phone was making a shrill fucking noise. At the present, he couldn't care less. Let it fucking ring.

Billy's mind was patchy. He remembered kicking the shit out of Jeannie and getting trashed. The thought of Jeff grabbing his meat was also at the front of his mind. After the vomit bath, everything went black. He didn't even have a clue how he'd gotten home.

Billy lay on the floor, eyes closed for another ten minutes. Rolling over and finding his phone was one of the hardest things he'd ever done. His brain was on fire; every sense inflamed, on code red.

He squinted at the cracked screen on his phone. There were 6 missed calls; 3 from Vin and 3 from Dillon. He clicked on Dillon's name and hit send.

Billy put the phone on speaker.

"Hello," Dillon said after the 4th ring.

"Yo, man," Billy said. He was staring up at the ceiling again, the phone laying on his chest.

Dillon was silent for a second and said, "You fucked up, Billy. For the last time."

Billy knew this was coming. The image of him puking into that fat bitch's mouth came back to him. He touched his pockets and found his pack of cigarettes. He popped one into his mouth. His dry, cracked lips wrapped around the filter as he lit it. The smoke didn't help his head, but he needed the nicotine. Another deep seeded feeling was creeping in, the feeling of heroin withdrawal.

"You're out of the band, Billy."

Billy went silent. A tendril of smoke rose from the tip of his cigarette. They couldn't fucking do that to him. He was the voice of *Shit Fist*, no one else. Since day one, he screamed and bled for the band. No fucking way they could cut him out.

"Did you fucking hear me, Billy? You're fucking out. *Shit Fist* is not yours anymore." Dillon's voice wavered. " *The Lucky Draw* took your Gibson too. To cover all of your damages." He paused. "Four fucking people are hospitalized from the chaos of your puke storm."

Billy didn't say anything. He just blew smoke rings in the air. They floated up without a care, dissipating against the peeling pain of the ceiling.

"Are you even listening to me?" Dillon asked.

Billy nodded, forgetting for a second he was on the phone. "Yeah," he croaked.

"They told everyone you had a stomach virus, but the stench of god only knows what kind of booze you drank, made it quite obvious. They ar-."

Billy had heard enough and hung up. He put the cigarette out on the floor.

"Jeannie," he yelled. No answer. "Jeannie," he

said again. "Get me a fucking glass of water." He knew she wasn't there, but he tried anyway. Slowly, on uneasy legs, he stood.

The room wavered and shook. His stomach lurched, another bubble of vomit crept into the back of his throat. This one he was able to keep in, swallowing it back down. It tasted like stew and vodka.

He stumbled to the sink and drank from the faucet in deep gulps. His belly sloshed with water and he felt slightly better. One problem down, now the big one; his withdrawal symptoms. He was clammy even though the windows were open to the fall morning. Billy's stomach was cramping and he knew he was going to have diarrhea. This could've been from the booze, but he knew the squirts was one of the many lovely symptoms of heroin withdrawal.

It was a photo finish, but Billy got on the bowl just in time to unleash a geyser of liquid shit. He felt it splash onto his cheeks and balls. No amount of wiping was going to clean this mess. This shit would require a shower.

Billy showered and put on semi-clean clothes and sat at the table. His pack of cigarettes was half empty, and he grabbed one. He had his head in his hands, mind racing on what to do. If he didn't get some dope in him soon he'd be in pain. Like a lightning bolt, an idea struck his drug addled brain.

Even though he was still sweating, he grabbed a jacket on his way out of the apartment. He didn't even bother locking the door.

※ ※ ※

The tattoo shop smelled like antiseptic and fresh paint. A relieving smell for customers who were letting strangers stab them with dozens of needles. It smelled clean, a scent he was unused to.

Original artwork hung on the walls. Pictures of abstract landscapes, terrifying monsters and those odd, geometric shapes. Billy looked around, the art was very impressive, as was the decor.

He was never one to decorate, but he could appreciate something nice. The walls were a calming mint green, with the canvasses of art strewn about. Plush brown leather couches flanked the door. Two small TVs were perched in the corners of the room. A glass counter separated the waiting area he was in and the actual tattoo booths in the back. He looked in the glass counter, which was pretty bare except for a few jars of post tattoo balm.

"Can I help you?" A voice said from behind the counter.

Billy, who was looking at the jars, didn't see or hear the woman approach. She moved like a spectre. He looked up at her and was taken aback.

In almost every tattoo parlor he'd stepped foot in, the female artists were less than attractive. Some were fuckable, but none were smokeshows like the one in front of him.

She was tall, almost as tall as him. Her black hair was pulled back in a loose ponytail, the way Jeannie used to put her hair before she sucked his dick. Dark eyes were outlined by a tasteful amount of black eye pencil. Her skin was porcelain and lips full. Her lips weren't the only full part about her. A ¾ sleeve, black sweater was taught over a perfect pair of large breasts. He didn't know how, but Billy knew she had her nipples pierced. He knew they'd be that perfect shade of pink, constantly taut with the thinnest stud through each one. His pants were getting tighter as he stiffened. He needed to get his mind off his cock between those tits, or his erection would be full and quite obvious.

For a second, Billy forgot why he was there. That was until a stomach cramp ripped through his body. He clenched his cheeks, just in case his body decided to release another blast of shit.

"Hi, ah, my name is Billy." He reached out to shake her hand. The cramp subsided, his stomach settling.

They touched and a smile lit up her face, making her more beautiful, if that was possible. Billy saw one of the geometric tattoos peeking from the sleeve of her shirt. He wondered what other treasures that sweater hid.

"Talia," she replied. Her hand was powder dry and cool. "What can I do for you, Billy?" She leaned on the counter.

"I spoke with," the guy's name was escaping him for a second, "Art," he blurted. "He said you guys were looking for paid volunteers for tattoos." Standing with her, he was self-conscious of his looks. He'd wished he would've brushed his hair after the shower. Instead he put it in a small ponytail. The back of his shirt was damp where it lay. His mustache was hanging just over his lip and his patchy beard looked like a mangy dog. He thought he was going to be dealing with Art, not this gothic beauty queen.

"Oh, yeah. He told me a cute guy stopped by," she said, color coming to her cheeks. She looked away.

Billy smiled at her and absently smoothed his hair. "Well, ah, here I am," he said, trying to be smooth. "So, how does this work? You pick the tat and just do it?"

Talia laughed. *Damn, even that's sexy*, Billy thought.

"Well, yeah," she said. "I've been out of the game for a few years and I want to have a little practice before we officially open."

A few years, he thought. *She couldn't be that old. If she was as old as me and had taken a few years off, she must've started in high school.*

"I'll give you $100 in hard, US currency for just a little of your skin," she said, a sly look in her eyes.

Something was going to be hard and it's not going to be the money, he thought. Billy knew he was going to have to jerk off when he got home or he'd explode.

"You can have whatever you want," he said, trying to keep the flirting alive, he hoped.

"Great," she said. "Let me just get the paperwork and I'll bring you back. I have the perfect piece for you."

"Yeah?" he asked.

Talia nodded. "Yup. I've been at this game for a while. I know people and just from the energy in your touch, I know just what you need."

Fuck, I'll give you more than a touch, if you want, Billy thought. He pictured himself eating her asshole and pussy like a melting ice cream cone. He was full blown hard now. Hopefully he could tuck it before he went back.

She walked away, Billy took the opportunity to look at her tight ass in her jeans. With deft hands that have had a lot of practice, Billy flipped his erection up, securing it in his waistband. Even with his endowment, this was the best option and hid it quite well.

"Here ya go," Talia said, coming back with a clipboard and paper.

Billy signed his name at the bottom without reading and handed it back to her.

"Follow me," she said, swinging her hips only the way a woman could.

"Anywhere," Billy said, smiling to himself.

Billy walked into her small studio. The wall was lined with more art, not on canvases, but thin, tracing paper. An architecture desk sat against the other side of the wall, a tablet and sketch pad lay on it. All of her inks were lined up like soldiers on three shelves above the desk.

"You can put your jacket on the table," she pointed to a table that was covered in wax paper, like the doctor's office.

Billy took his jacket off. His *Everwar* band t-shirt, one of his favorite local bands, was fading, but he'd never get rid of it. It was too comfortable.

"Take a seat," she pointed to an antique barber chair.

He did. The old leather felt soft and comfortable.

"So, any preference of location?" She eyed him up. "I was thinking about the upper right arm." She stared at him.

Billy was suddenly self-conscious of his track marks. His favorite spot to shoot up was in his right arm. He saw Talia looking at the scab.

"Blood donation," he said, blushing, hoping his voice stayed neutral. Even he wouldn't believe the lie. Hopefully she did. "So, upper, right," he said, rolling up his sleeve. His only tattoo was on his back, so the rest of him was wide open.

Talia touched his arm, lightly, almost tracing the lines of his bicep. "Looks good to me," she said.

"Let's get started." She rolled his sleeve up, securing it with a couple pieces of Scotch tape. She grabbed a disposable razor from a jar and dry shaved the few hairs he had. After he was smooth, she wiped him down with alcohol, which stung his freshly shaved skin. She put a thin layer of ointment on his skin, making it glisten.

"Do I get to see the design first?" he asked.

She looked at him, a devilish glimmer in her eye. "Don't you want to be surprised?" She asked, slipping black, rubber gloves on.

"Eh, fuck it. Go for it," he said, watching her pour inks into little plastic thimbles. She put a small amount of ointment on the bottom of each, keeping them secure to the paper towels she'd laid down.

The machine chattered to life and she plunged the needle into black ink. "Ready?" she asked.

She's going to freehand this whole thing? He asked himself. *Luckily I can hide this if it turns out like shit.*

Billy nodded.

The needle bit into his flesh and away they went.

He was intoxicated with the smell of her. Her

hair was fresh and clean, but there was a hint of something else in it. Something earthy and almost animalistic. Billy had to take a few deep breaths to keep himself under control. If he hardened again, there would be no hiding it. It might work in his favor or he might end up with a half finished tattoo and blue balls.

The needle stabbed and he bled, but it was almost blissful. He'd never had a tattoo like this. Something about her touch was angelic. They made small talk, but for the life of him, he couldn't remember any of it.

The machine danced back and forth. Each wipe of the paper towel revealed more and more. He watched the lines, perfectly straight, form odd shapes in his skin. Of course, she chose a geometric pattern. Billy didn't know what the fuck it was, but it was cool looking. Maybe he wouldn't have to cover it.

"All done," she said, the chatter of the machine stopping abruptly. Talia sprayed it with a cooling liquid and wiped it down. Fresh drops of blood and ink rose out. She gave it another wipe. "Take a look," she said, pointing towards a full-length mirror.

Billy stood. It looked great. He admired it,

turning his arm so he could see it from every angle. It was like nothing he'd ever seen. Three circles, each smaller as they descended his arm, sat on top of each other. Inside each one were various symbols made up of crisscrossing lines. Each symbol was similar, but distinctly different. One looked like a face, but only at a certain angle. The others were completely random, or so Billy thought.

"It looks," Billy realized he felt pretty good. His withdrawal symptoms had dulled, more of an afterthought. "Amazing," he finally said.

"Yay," she said, clapping her gloved hands together. "Ok, sit down and let me clean you up and get a few pics."

Billy listened.

Talia applied a generous amount of balm and snapped a few pictures with her phone. She wrapped his arm in plastic wrap and pulled her gloves off.

"All set," she said, standing up. She grabbed her pants and wiggled her hips, pulling them up.

Billy put his jacket on and stood there for a second, as if waiting.

"Oh, shit. My bad," she said, grabbing her purse from under the desk. She pulled out 5 crisp $20 bills. "I'm not used to paying to tattoo someone," she giggled.

Billy felt guilty, but took the money. It disappeared into his pocket. "Yeah, I'm sure it feels weird, but you're really good. I'm sure once you fully open, this place will be a hit."

Talia gestured towards the door.

Billy walked towards it, she was right behind him. He could see through the glass doors night had fallen. God damn time change.

As if she could read his mind, she said, "Time flies when you're having fun."

Billy laughed. "Yeah, I guess so." He held out his hand. "Thanks. I'm sure I'll see you around."

Talia shook his hand. "Until next time, Billy Silver," she whispered.

Billy walked out, wondering when he'd given her his last name.

Talia watched him go. A car drove by, hitting its brakes. For just a second, her eyes lit up red. She smiled.

❋ ❋ ❋

Billy put the Chinese food on the table. He grabbed a fork and dug in. He was starving. It was probably from the adrenaline dump of getting tattooed, but he thought just being around a healthy and attractive person was the real reason.

Jeannie still hadn't come back, but Billy didn't give a shit if he ever saw her again.

Billy opened his beer, the first in the six pack and drank it down. Shockingly, he didn't want any dope. It was like he was clean. Even the beer wasn't hitting the spot like it usually did. He finished his dinner, choosing water over beer, to wash it down.

He walked into the bathroom and removed the plastic wrap from the tattoo. It was bloody, but it still looked great. His mind wandered back to Talia and the erection he had in the shop was making its return.

A few minutes later, Billy was watching his cum swirl down the toilet bowl.

He threw on a pair of shorts, plugged his phone in and for the first time in a long time, went to bed at a reasonable time.

His dreams were vast and unnatural. Horrifying and at the same time, pleasurable. He dreamed of violence, pain and rape. Gouts of blood, piles of shit and dead bodies everywhere. Even in sleep, he could smell it.

Dream Billy had his flaccid penis in one hand and a filet knife in the other. With the first swipe of the blade, he cut the root of his cock. Blood oozed, but there was no pain. He put the blade into the deep slice and slashed again. This one did it. In his hand he held his bleeding, severed manhood. Then he felt hungry. Luckily for Dream Billy, there was a crackling, hot frying pan. He put his member in the pan, watching it flop and sizzle. He salivated like a dog. Billy grabbed it from the pan, half raw, and tore into it. His testicles popped when he bit, like those cream eggs you get during Easter.

His grotesque meal was over, but his body was already revolting. He squatted down and shit on the floor. Hunger pangs hit him again, and to his dismay, he began scooping up and eating his hot excrement. It tasted great.

There was no heroin in this dream, so Billy made due with another chemical; bleach. He injected it into his veins, which were fat and welcoming. The burn was unbearable and almost orgasmic.

His eye sockets fit his thumbs perfectly. He knew they would. Billy pressed, softly at first, admiring the starbursts in his black vision. Galaxies rose and fell the harder he pressed. His eyes popped under his thumbs, everything full of delicious pain. He dug in deeper, felt warmth over his thumbs. His darkness was complete.

Even blind, he still hunted for torment. His hunger had returned and nothing he ate seemed to sate it.

The sound of a mewling baby drew him. With ocular fluid and blood streaking his face, he used his ears to find the baby. His hands touched dewy baby hair on its soft scalp. Billy picked the baby up, cradling it. Ravenously, he bit into its stomach. The baby shrieked and screamed, music to his ears. He ate and ate, loops of intestines dangling from his mouth. Every crunch brought the taste of blood and shit. It was a 4 star meal.

Bloated, bloody and now horny, Billy sat down. Glumly, he remembered he'd chopped his dick off. He reached down to the bloody hole where it used to be. To his delight, it had grown back and was standing at attention. He smiled as he rubbed it, using blood as lube.

"Billy Silver," a throaty female voice said.

"Who the fuck is that?" he said, his bloody eye sockets looking around. He didn't take his hand off of his cock.

"Oh, Billy, you know who it is," Talia said. "Let me take care of that."

Billy felt her hand, powder dry and cool, wrap around his member.

She stroked it and without warning, put it in her mouth.

He groaned, the heat of her mouth alighting his senses. He wished his eyes would've grown back, so he could watch the performance. If he knew what was actually sucking his dick, he would've died of fright.

"How's that feel?" she grumbled. Her angelic voice sounded like gravel.

"Fucking amazing. Keep it going and I'll blow."

She laughed, "Oh, not yet," she stroked him. "I want that inside me."

He felt her straddle him, and could sense it. The smell of her cunt was burning his nostrils. Billy breathed it in, wanted to taste it. She obliged his unspoken request, pressing her genitals to his face. His tongue played inside of her. Pussy juice, viscous and sour, dripped down his bloodied chin.

"Now, for the grand finale," she growled, pulling away from his face.

Billy kept trying to lick, like an animal feeding from its mother's breast. She grabbed his dick and sat on it, plunging deeper until the whole thing was inside. He lay there, motionless as she rode him. His orgasm was in the periphery. He wanted to shoot so badly, but didn't want this to end.

"You like that?" she said, her voice deeper.

Billy whined, the sound of sex loud in his ears. No, this wasn't sex. Sex was something married people did once a week. A couple of pathetic pumps with a half flaccid dick, into an ungroomed ax wound of a cunt, until a dribble of cum spurted out. No, this was fucking. This was rutting. They were animals and they were mating.

He was getting ready to blast his hot load into her. With unsteady hands, he blindly reached up, wanting to grab her nipple piercings as he came. Instead of perfect tits he found fur. Coarse fur covered heavy muscles. The odor of livestock assaulted him.

"What the fuck?" he shouted. Billy tried to buck this creature off of him, but just thrust deeper. Then, to his dismay, he felt something probing at his asshole.

She laughed, fucking him harder. "Are you going to cum for me?"

He was, whether he liked it or not. Something thick and heavy forced its way between his clenched ass cheeks. He struggled to keep it out of him, but his asshole wasn't strong enough. Billy screamed as his anus tore. The phallic object split him. Hot blood poured out of his destroyed ass as it burrowed deeper into him. All of the pleasure he felt earlier, was gone. His injuries lit pain receptors on fire. A savage scream erupted from his throat and a thick rope of semen pumped out of his cock into the demon's pussy.

Billy sat up, his dream drifted away. He was sweating and realized his underwear stuck to him. For a second he thought he'd pissed himself and then he felt the sliminess of semen. He knew he was having a hot dream, but it was only on the fringes of his memory. He hadn't had a wet dream in a long time, but the orgasm still echoed through his body.

He staggered into the bathroom and cleaned himself. He put on his shorts without underwear and lay back down. The dream was erased from his memory as he drifted back to sleep.

CHAPTER 4

Three days after getting her face kicked in by Billy, Jeannie was starting to feel better. She sat on the edge of the hotel room bed, a cigarette in her hand. The TV was turned to some trashy daytime show, but she wasn't truly watching. Her mind wandered, but always came back to the same thing; heroin.

T-Rex had loaned her a bundle and put her up in the hotel room the night she left Billy. She knew it wasn't out of the kindness of his heart. She owed him a debt and was expected to pay it off. Her only discernible skill was cock gobbling, so that's what she did.

She would suck and fuck whoever he told her to and he kept her fed, sheltered and high. It was better than getting tuned up by Billy.

Jeannie put her cigarette out and walked into the bathroom. Her face was a bruised and swollen mess. Shades of yellow, purple and green adorned her cheeks. She smiled, split lips stretching painfully. Her broken tooth throbbed. Every cock that went down her throat was painful. At least the johns all wore condoms, so she didn't get any cum in her mouth. The only one who refused was Deet, but he stopped cumming in her mouth when she almost puked on his balls.

Her rig sat on the small vanity. She had two bags of dope left. Hopefully, if she made enough tonight, T-Rex would give her another bundle. She shook one bag, ever so carefully, onto a spoon. She sucked water into her needle and put a few drops onto the narcotic. With deft fingers, she picked up the spoon, heating the bottom of it with her lighter. Jeannie put a piece of cotton ball in the spoon to act as a rudimentary filter. She placed the needle against the cotton and drew it back, sucking the tan liquid into the reserve.

She walked back to the bed and sat.

"Which little piggy is gonna get it today?" she asked herself. "This little piggy went to market," she said, wiggling her big toe. "This little piggy stayed home," the next toe. "This little piggy had roast beef," she paused. "And heroin," she said, slipping the needle through old scar tissue. The drug hit her like a truck.

Was this a hot bag? She thought. Sometimes when dealers are cutting their dope, they miss one, leaving it mostly pure. Even a seasoned pro like Jeannie could overdose on a hot bag, especially if there was fentanyl in it.

Jeannie fell asleep, not caring if it was the end. Death couldn't hurt as bad as life.

※ ※ ※

Jeannie awoke to a pounding on the door.

"Ay, wake the fuck up," T-Rex yelled at the door. He hit it again. "Get your skank ass up and open the fucking door."

She snapped awake. *That bag wasn't that hot,* she thought. With the back of her hand she wiped the drool from her cheek.

"Coming," she groaned. She threw the deadbolt and the door flew open.

"Where the fuck you been?" T-Rex said. He stunk of marihuana. Deet was behind him, blocking the whole doorway.

Jeannie saw it was dark outside. She must've slept the entire day, instead of selling herself on the street. She'd have to make it up tonight, which she hated. The chances of getting raped were much worse at night, plus it was fucking freezing out.

"Sorry," she murmured. Her swollen lips made talking awkward. She thought he was going to hit her, but he never did.

"No matter. I need you tonight anyway," he said, lighting a cigarette. "You still got that birth control thing in your snatch?" He asked, flicking ashes in the ashtray on the window sill.

"Yeah, but everyone wears rubbers anyway. No breaks so far," she said, looking around for a cigarette.

"Here," he handed her one of his.

"Thanks," she said, using his offered lighter. He was being nice and immediately her defenses went up. In her life, whenever men were nice to her, they wanted something. That something was usually sexual in some way. Her instincts were right.

"My boy is in the porn industry and his actress fell through. He needs a fill in for tonight. I told him I had the perfect girl." He stared at her, trying to catch her eye. "Don't I?"

Jeannie looked at him. "Who do I have to

fuck? Do I have to go raw or is it with a rubber?"

He ashed his smoke, "It's a gangbang. Not a big one, just 3 guys, but it's all creampies. They're all clean. Just wanted to make sure you weren't getting pregnant."

She looked at him apprehensively. "I'm not sure. I've never done that before and what if they are lying and I get something?"

His kind look melted away. He slapped the cigarette out of her mouth. It smoldered on the bedspread.

"I take you in, feed you, get you high and this is how you repay me? Get your shit and get the fuck out!" He yelled, pointing at the door.

"No, no," she said, panicking. "I didn't say no, I was just thinking out loud. Yeah, of course I'll do it. What's my cut?"

She might not be the smartest, but she even knew if she was getting fucked it was for money.

T-Rex smiled at her. "Atta girl. $100 and 2 bundles."

Her eyes lit up. "Sounds good to me," she said, thinking of the dope.

"Good. They'll be here in 2 hours. Go wash your pussy and throw some makeup on." He walked out of the room without another word.

* * *

The last 3 days had been the best in Billy's recent life. He woke early every day and took a walk to Downing Park. The day after his tattoo, he bought a scratch off and won $500. Normally, he would've spent that on dope and booze, but since the tattoo, he didn't feel like he needed them. It was as if the ink cured him. Hell, he was barely smoking anymore either. He took his lottery money and went to the pawn shop.

Cue Ball pawn shop was what you'd expect in a shitty little city: cheap jewelry, outdated electronics and video games. Billy looked around. He'd hope to find his Gibson, but had no luck. He grabbed a solid looking acoustic guitar and tested the tune. It sounded pretty good and the strings were tight.

Billy brought it up to the counter, which had a wall of bulletproof glass in front of it. The price on the guitar was $75, but the layer of dust suggested it had been around for a while.

"Would you take $50 for this?" Billy asked,

holding up the guitar.

The clerk, who appeared less than thrilled to be dealing with anyone, looked him over.

"$60 and it's yours," he said, scratching his cheek.

Billy looked at the glass case in front of him. It held knives and other weapons. He saw a knife that had metal knuckles for a handle. A nasty looking piece of weaponry.

"Throw in the knuckle knife and you have a deal."

The clerk took the knife out. "This is illegal in NY. It's strictly a show piece." He handed it to Billy through a small cutout in the glass.

Billy slid $60 to him. "Yeah, sure. I'll hang it right above the fireplace." There was no sheath, so he just tucked under his belt. He felt like a pirate.

He walked back home and took a seat at the table. He kicked his shoes off and started playing the guitar.

"Ah, fuck," he said, stopping the strings with his hand. His tattoo, which was pretty much healed, burned like hell. He got up and headed towards the bathroom.

An urge started rising in him, the urge to snap his toe. He didn't know why, but the feeling was akin to shivering from withdrawal and having a full needle of dope in his hand. Dying of thirst and someone handing you a pitcher of ice water. He needed to do it, yearned to, just to satisfy the feeling. Before he could even comprehend the desire to hurt himself, he acted. Billy smashed his pinky toe into the doorframe, snapping it like a twig.

"Fuck!" He yelled, stumbling into the bathroom. He sat on the toilet lid, nearly cracking it. His toe was crooked and already bruised. Billy broke his arm when he was a teenager, but he didn't remember it hurting like this. He touched it gingerly. Pain shot up his leg. "Motherless fuck," he mumbled. Did he really think it would've felt good? Something in his head said it would. Something compelled him. Stubbing your toe is nature's 'fuck you' but snapping it is even worse.

He stood, favoring his toe, and opened the medicine cabinet. There wasn't much; old cough syrup (alcohol free, or he would've drank it a long time ago) Jeannie's yeast infection medication (she really did have a nasty pussy) and a roll of tape. Billy grit his teeth and straightened out his toe. He wrapped it against the one next to it. Sweat coated his head. The pain made his balls suck against his body.

He lifted his sleeve to look at the tattoo. It looked completely normal. He expected to see it red and inflamed, but the skin was healed.

Billy limped his way back into the living room and turned his head towards the window. It was shut, but he could've sworn he'd smelled the distinct odor of livestock. The phantom smell disappeared as quick as it had come. His eyes then caught the guitar. Billy picked it up and began playing again.

Before he knew it, an hour had gone by. The tips of his fingers hurt, but in a good way. Like he'd accomplished something. He put the guitar down and walked over to the window. He opened it and took out a cigarette. Something peculiar caught his eye on the street below him. A black dog was chasing a cat.

They ran around a parked car, the dog always one step behind, but closing. The cat ran under the car and Billy lost it. The dog did something Billy had never seen before, it smacked a bottle at the cat. The cat, seeing the bottle come after it, ran. The dog broke as soon as it hit the bottle, guessing which way the cat was going to go. It guessed right. The mangy, black dog grabbed the cat by its back. The cat screamed, almost human sounding, and thrashed. Corded muscles flexed under the dog's black fur as it thrashed the dying cat. It smashed the cat into the curb, breaking its neck sideways. The dog started in at the cat's soft stomach, powerful jaws opening the gut. With a mouthful of entrails, the dog looked up at Billy. Its eyes were red.

"Ow, fuck," Billy said, breaking his gaze with the dog. His wrist was blistering and he noticed he was burning himself with his lighter instead of lighting his cigarette. He ran to the sink, limping still, and ran his arm under cold water. What the fuck was he doing? First his toe, now his wrist.

The burn still hurt like hell, but the pain faded some. Billy went back to the window to look for the weird dog, but both animals were gone.

❊ ❊ ❊

Billy had a burger and fries for dinner, avoiding any more injuries. He thought about it the rest of the day. The burning of his tattoo and the urge to break his fucking toe. It was almost as bad as his lust for dope, which had all but gone. He did snort a little bump, just to dull the pain.

He lay in bed, thinking about the dream he had the night before. For the life of him, he couldn't remember it. He just remembered waking up with an oyster in his underwear. Billy slept, sliding into that dreamworld once again.

Even though he didn't remember the other one, he felt like this one was better. He was in a candy store. The intoxicating smell of sugar made his sweet tooth throb.

"You can have anything you'd like," said Talia. She was dressed like an old-time soda jerk. She walked behind the counter.

Billy looked at everything. "Ah, it all looks so good," he said. "Just give me one of everything." He said.

"Coming right up," she said. Her uniform beautifully framed her ass in a pair of black pants.

Billy took a seat on one of the stools. Old soda fountains glimmered in the overhead lights.

"Here ya go," she handed him a plate of assorted sweets.

"Thanks a bunch," he said, picking up a huge gummy worm. It was a confectionary dream. He chewed, the blissful sugar giving him a high. "Delicious," he mumbled, grabbing a handful of sweets, shoving them all in his mouth. He chomped, wishing he had a drink. "Hey, howabout a soda?" He asked.

She grinned at him, "Howabout a water bottle of vodka instead?" She asked, this time in Jeff's voice.

Billy stared at her, her mouth widening into an almost lupine grin.

"Hey, get the fuck out of here!" she yelled at the door, still in Jeff's voice.

Billy snapped his head towards the door. The black dog stood there, his muzzle slick with blood. He let out a throaty growl, his yellow teeth exposed.

"Let me suck it and I'll give you the whole damn thing," Talia said in Jeff's voice.

Billy turned back to the bar. Jeff stood there.

"Come on, you fucking faggot! Let me suck it!" he growled at Billy. He flicked his tongue out and bit down. His tongue severed, blood oozed from his mouth. "Blood is the best lube," he slurred.

Billy, unconsciously took a bite of another sweet. It was a gummy tongue. As he bit, blood burst in his mouth. He heard a growl behind him, just before yellow teeth sunk into his neck.

Billy woke up in pain. His mouth tasted of

copper. Reflexively he put his hand over it. He ran into the bathroom and spit into the sink. A stub of pink flesh and blood rested in the porcelain. His stomach dropped; he knew what it was. Billy opened his mouth, looking in the medicine cabinet mirror. He'd bitten off the tip of his tongue.

※ ※ ※

The same time Billy was spitting out the chunk of his tongue, Jeannie was on all fours, getting fucked.

One guy pounded her asshole, which had started bleeding. The other violently fucked her in the mouth. The third, well he couldn't hold his nut as well as the other two. He had pumped a few times in her freshly shaved cunt and blew it. Luckily he told the camera man and they were able to get the mess as he pulled out.

The director got the attention of his two male actors and tapped his watch. It was time for the money shots.

The guy on Jeannie's face started thrusting like a madman. She had enough heroin in her, she was numb and barely gagged as he assaulted her throat. Without warning he pulled out and jerked his dick twice before cumming on her face and hair. The first big spurt hit her left eye. As she was blinking it out, the guy in her asshole unleashed what felt like a gallon of jizz. The warmth leaked out of her. He pulled out quickly, a cum fart followed.

"Zoom in on her asshole," the director said to his cameraman. "Hey, just stay on all fours for a second longer," he said to Jeannie.

She could hear the shitty semen leaking out of her onto the bed spread.

"Cut," he said. "Ok boys, wipe your cocks and let's go." He lit up a thin cigarette. "We'll settle with Rex," he said to Jeannie, who lay face down on the bed in a stupor.

They left without another word. The cum in her hair dried to a crunchy consistency. She wanted to shoot up again, but she was afraid to move. Her asshole was on fire. It felt like she'd been fucked with a hot iron. Slowly, the dope in her system lulled her sleep. She dreamt of nothing.

* * *

Billy woke up the following morning feeling like he chugged acid. His tongue was swollen to twice its size. Reluctantly, he got up off the futon and went to the kitchen sink. The last thing he wanted was an infection, but he knew his next decision was going to hurt like a bitch. Billy dumped a healthy amount of salt into a glass and filled it with warm water. His heart pounded with anticipation. It was going to burn, but part of him looked forward to it. He took a mouthful, relishing the burn, and swished it around. The pain from the night before returned, his abused nerves were relit with agony. He spit the blood streaked water onto a pile of unwashed dishes.

Billy leaned on the sink, sweat popping up on his forehead. He turned around and sat at his table. There was still half a bag of dope laying there. He needed something to take the edge off the pain. Billy limped into the bathroom; his toe still protested. He found his rig next to the sink and grabbed it.

With deft hands, he tied the rubber tube around his arm, making his veins pop. The rest of the heroin was in the spoon and within seconds, it was in the needle.

His tattoo began burning again. This time he ignored it, knowing his injuries needed a little medicine to quiet their barking. He sunk the hypo into his vein. The pain started to dull, but it was still ever present.

Slowly, he brought the tip of the needle up to his face. *I wonder what this would feel like in my eyeball,* he thought. The needle was getting closer. There would be a satisfying little 'pop' when it went into the outer layer of eye. He smiled at the thought.

"What the fuck am I doing?" he said aloud, taking the needle from his face. *No, not your eyeball. How would you be able to see the torment?* His thoughts felt almost alien, as if someone else was thinking with his mind.

The urge to hurt himself was back and stronger than ever. No, not his eyeball, but his nail bed would do. Just the right amount of delicious pain, but not causing any real damage.

Billy wanted to fight his hand, but couldn't. He slid the needle under the nail on his left pointer finger. The hypo was dark against his pink skin. The pain was electric, but after a little resistance, Billy sunk it all the way. The tip slid out from the nail, poking his cuticle. Ever so slowly, he pulled it out. An angry red line formed under his nail.

He wept with pain and pleasure. Unfortunately, the desire didn't go away. Luckily, he had 9 more fingers.

* * *

Billy walked. After the episode with the needle, he was terrified. The pain was like nothing he'd ever felt and some part of him needed it. It was his drug, his new addiction. His body didn't care about heroin or booze, it needed pain and it was going to get it.

He planned on going to the local pharmacy for some pain killers, but instead he walked aimlessly. He needed to get out of the apartment. There were too many things he could use to hurt himself. In a way, it didn't matter. If the urge came back, he'd satisfy it.

Billy entered Downing Park, one of the few nice areas in the city.

The park had a decent size pond, that was usually inhabited by local ducks and geese. They shit everywhere, but so did some of the people. Old men and kids would fish the pond, snatching blue gills, perch and the occasional bass. A large hill sat at the center of the park, with a parking area at the top.

The morning was beautifully sunny, with just a hint of a breeze to rattle the leaves. Billy walked by the pond. An old black man, who probably lived in this city when it was a nice place to live, sat on a bench, reading a newspaper. He was sharply dressed, the way only old men could be. He wore brown slacks, with a brown tweed coat and matching hat. His fishing pole leaned against the bench. The red and white bobber floated on the calm surface of the pond.

Billy wondered what eating a fish hook would feel like. *Would I shit it out*? He thought. *No, probably not. It would get tangled, ripping its way along my gut. Some doctor would have to yank it out. I wonder if they could do it without anesthesia?* His tattoo was starting to burn again. He wanted to cry.

Billy ran up the hill, burning his lungs and legs. Hopefully the pain in his legs would sate his lust for pain. He stopped under a maple tree, which had lost most of its leaves. His stomach cramped as he leaned over. Stars formed in his eyes as his body tried to recover from the burst of exercise. It was definitely not used to that. His subconscious request wasn't answered. The desire remained.

Something flew past his head, narrowly missing his hair.

"What the fuck?" Billy looked around. A fat robin flew away from him, but it turned around for another run. The bird came screeching in like a dive bomber, aimed right at him. He ducked, swatting at it. "What did I do to you?" He asked the bird, as if it would reply. Something had the bird pissed off, but Billy didn't know what he could've done. It's not like she had eggs or hatchlings, it was fall. Whatever he'd done, this bird was out for him. Again she swooped down, angry and fierce.

The urge still burned, but there was something new in it. Something different. A fresh way to quiet his desire. The bird let out another shriek and this time she hit Billy. She became tangled in his hair. He grabbed her with his right hand. She was wrapped tight and when Billy pulled, she came out with a clump of his hair. She pecked furiously, her sharp beak bringing forth little drops of blood with every attack. Each one was painfully sublime.

"Oh, you stupid little twat," he said to the bird. He could feel her bones shifting under grasp. The bird struggled, pecking him as he squeezed. Each peck brought out tiny pools of blood. Her attack became weaker as he crushed her frail bones. His hand stung, but the pain was lovely. Her eyes bulged and shrieks stopped. Thin bones fractured as he squeezed. One slid into his palm. She was dead, but Billy kept going. Delicate little eyes popped out, dangling by optic nerves. He looked at her upclose. The urge was gone. He felt great. The corpse fell from his hand; a nighttime snack for a possum...or a black dog.

The feeling of relief was fading, but something new replaced it. Fear.

CHAPTER 5

Dillon tapped his drumsticks together. On the third hit, the band kicked off in a torrent of noise. He pounded away on his drums, sweat dripped as he kept the beat going. His hands and feet were a blur and he felt electric. The soon-to-be new lead singer of *Shit Fist*, Aaron, belted out the lyrics to the song, *Self-Made Abortionist*.

"Now you feel it, my hanger is deep! I told you slut, to suck my meat!" He growled the last lyric, almost identical to Billy. Actually, he was better than Billy. "Your pussy stinks, like old piss! Luckily I'm a self-made abortionist!" The last word drew out with the whine of the guitar.

The song ended. Aaron breathed heavy into the microphone. He was smiling.

"How was that?" he turned around, asking his new band mates.

Vin let his bass hang. "Dude, you fucking killed it," he said, setting his bass down. He pulled a cigarette pack from his shirt pocket.

"Second that," said Dillon, sipping a bottle of water.

Sammy, the other guitar player, said, "Like nothing I've ever heard. We should've dumped Billy years ago."

Aaron smiled, knowing the job was his. He loved singing and the rough music and graphic lyrics of *Shit Fist* were right up his alley. He studied them for hours and listened to live recordings, just to get it right.

"Thanks guys, I really appreciate it. I've been looking for a solid band for years and I think I've found it."

They echoed his sentiment.

"Do you mind if we do *IV bag full of piss* next? I really want to nail the chorus."

Vin put his cigarette out. "Sounds good to me. *The Lucky Draw* is giving us another shot in two nights and I want it to be perfect."

This was news to Aaron. He knew the band played a lot of shows, but since Billy's last performance, he didn't anticipate any gigs in the near future. Hell, he didn't even know if they were going to hire him. He was ecstatic.

"What do you say, Aaron? Do you want to sing lead for *Shit Fist*?" Vin asked.

Aaron looked at the others, who were all nodding.

"Fuck yeah," he said, shaking each of their hands. "I can't wait to melt some fucking faces," he said.

"Let's get it going," Dillon said when Aaron took his place back on the mic. He tapped his sticks.

* * *

Hours later, closer to dark, Billy still had feathers under his nails. They were stuck in sticky blood, but he really didn't care.

After his slaughter of the bird, Billy felt great. Rejuvenated even. The urge to hurt himself or anyone else was gone. For the time being. It didn't take the pain away from the numerous injuries he'd sustained, but he didn't care. He finished his trek to the pharmacy, buying a huge bottle of acetaminophen. He took 4, dry swallowing them when he left the store. The rest of the day was pretty uneventful.

He had a lunch consisting of a bag of chips, soda and ice cream sandwich. Then, the rain came. It was one of those cold, October showers. A few degrees colder and the city would've been whitewashed in snow.

Billy spent the remainder of the day at home, watching shitty tv. He smoked cigarette after cigarette, mainly to just kill time. He played his guitar for a little while, but even that felt bland. Something was missing.

Billy pulled his chair over to the window and opened it. The night sounds of the city were washed out by the deluge. He strained his eyes at the pool of butter colored light from the street-lamp. For a second, he thought he saw the black dog. Billy blew smoke out the window, focusing.

"Just a bag," he said to himself, realizing the black figure was a garbage bag. He flicked the butt into the rainy night. His arm started to burn. Absently, he brushed at himself, thinking he'd dropped ashes on his skin. But it was the tattoo which burned him.

Billy rose and walked over to the table. He looked lovingly at the knuckle knife; the way he used to look at a hypo full of dope. It fit perfectly in his grasp, like it was made for him. The edge looked razor sharp, even though Billy was sure it was a cheap Chinese knock-off. That line of shiny steel called to him. It sung to his flesh; craving his blood, or just any blood.

Come on, Billy, the knife said to him. *Just let me taste that sweet, sweet blood.*

He was cracking up. There was no way a knife was talking to him. But, the blade did have a point. How nice would it be to feel that steel slide through meat? The warmth of blood on his hand. Exquisite.

Billy put his left hand on the table. He set the edge of the knife against the first knuckle of his pointer finger. Slowly, and as gentle as a virgin lover, he drew the blade back. He was right, it was razor sharp. The cut was so clean, he saw the skin part, all the way to the bone, before the blood even came. A thin red line welled up and ran over his finger-nail, which sported old blood from his prodding with the needle earlier.

I bet I can cut it right off, he thought. That, now that was a dandy fucking idea. Billy put the blade back in the fresh cut. He pushed. The ligament holding that first knuckle cut cleanly, almost as if it weren't there. Billy sliced, harder this time. Before he knew it, the blade was cutting into the table.

Blood oozed from the stump. Billy shivered in pain, delicious pain. The craving was diminished, but far from satisfied. His blood was good, but he needed something better. He had an idea of where he could find it.

* * *

Robert "Gypsy" Atkinson, lay in an old, kid's sleeping bag on the floor of an abandoned, half burned garage. His worldly possessions; a tattered bookbag, a large thermos, a deck of cards with naked women on them and assorted little knick-knacks, lay on an old milk crate. The street-light had finally been repaired, lighting his little room. He hated using batteries for his flashlight, but when he needed to, he did.

Gypsy was 66 years old and had lived in Newburgh his entire life. For the last 25 of those years, he was homeless. He never messed with drugs (maybe some weed here or there, but not the hard stuff) but was a sucker for booze. This and his love of gambling led him to the streets.

If he was being honest, which he usually was, he didn't mind it. The young bucks, that's what he called the majority of the residents in the city, didn't mess with him. He was an OG, an original gangster, even though he'd never been in a gang. When he was freshly homeless, he'd stabbed a man in the neck with a knife during a dice game. That man didn't die, but the bloody attack gained the small man street credit. People were nice to him, even in a notoriously violent city. Young bucks would let him sip from their bottles (a nip for the Gyp, he'd always say) from time to time, and even buy him one of his own. Restaurant owners would set food that was designated as trash in a plastic bag and leave it on top of the dumpster.

All things considered, life was pretty good. Gypsy found his current residence over a year prior. The garage had been set on fire in an insurance scam by the owner. Unfortunately for him, the fire department was just around the block, returned from another call. They spotted the smoke before the call even came in. The fire, assisted by copious amounts of gas, tore through the building. The fire department was able to knock it down, but the building was lost. It didn't take a rocket scientist to figure out it was clearly arson. The owner was arrested and had yet to return.

Gypsy, who would stay where he could, found the building. The smoke smell didn't bother him and he made it his own.

The street-light gave him enough light to read by. The worn detective paperback was folded on itself. Gypsy's watery eyes moved, mouthing every word. Something he did since he was young.

His watch died last year, but he knew it was getting late.

"Goddamn, Gyp," he said to himself. "Getch'yo ass to bed." He closed the book and took off his glasses. They were only readers, but they were better than nothing. He put them on his milk crate and curled up in the sleeping bag.

❋ ❋ ❋

Billy stood outside the old garage. The blacktop was wavy from the heat of the fire. Dead weeds peeked out of the cracks. Glass glittered in the street-light, like a blanket of diamonds. A fresh condom, the tip still full of cum, lay dangling just above the sewer drain. Billy saw all of this, and didn't. His mind was focused on one thing.

The rain fell in sheets. He was the only one on the street, not that he would've cared. He had an itch that needed scratching.

Billy tapped on the window near Gypsy's head.

"Hey, Gyp," Billy said, his voice drowned out by the rain. He tapped again. *Maybe the old fucker wasn't home,* Billy thought. "It's Silver Dollar," he said.

Billy had met the old man about a year ago. They weren't exactly friends, but they did talk if they ran into each other. Gypsy quickly gave Billy the nickname "Silver Dollar" and it stuck with the old man.

Gypsy's old, wrinkled face popped up in the window. Billy thought he looked like a California raisin. The old man was clean shaven, just a little gray mustache. He had a few gray hairs, but they were barely noticeable.

Gypsy didn't open the window, but instead pointed towards the backdoor.

Billy nodded and walked over.

"Silver Dollar, what in the shit are you doing out on a night like this?" The bitter tang of urea hit Billy full force. He was pretty sure the old man routinely pissed himself.

Billy had his finger bandaged and pulled his injured hand out of his pocket, showing the old bum.

"My fucking old lady went off the deep end," he said. His hoodie was soaked through. He looked and felt miserable. There was another, and much stronger feeling in the foreground of his consciousness. "Cut my fucking hand. I took off, knowing I didn't want to fuck her up and get locked up."

Gypsy handed him a threadbare towel.

Billy took it with revulsion and wrapped himself in it. "Thanks, Gyp," he said. "I didn't come empty handed." He opened the towel and pulled a bottle of cheap vodka from his hoodie pocket. "A nip for the Gyp."

The old man took the bottle, looking at it like fucking Golem at the ring.

"My man, Silver Dollar, comes through." He said, twisting off the cap and taking a big swig. He shivered from the burn of alcohol. "Ah, that's good," he said, smacking his lips together. "Say, you don't have any weed with you, do you?"

Billy only smoked marihuana once in his life. When he was 14 years old, his buddy and he rolled a shitty joint and smoked it in his backyard. Unknown to Billy, his father came home early and caught them. His friend ran, but Billy had nowhere to run. His father beat the shit out of him, broke his arm. "No son of mine is gonna smoke grass," he said, wrenching Billy's arm behind his back. "I am not having it in my house. Fucking grass!" He spat, just as Billy's arm snapped. The sound, like a pine knot in the fire, made his father drop him to the ground, where Billy sobbed. They had told his mother he took a nasty spill on his bike, to try and cover the arm and bruises on his face. She pretended to buy it, but they both knew she didn't. It was never spoken of again.

"Sorry, Gyp. I have a cigarette, if you want one." Billy said, hoping his pack was dry.

Gypsy took another healthy swig and said, "Sure, sure. A little non-wacky tobacky is just fine."

Billy held out a surprisingly dry cigarette. *Last smoke of a condemned man,* he thought.

"Thank you," Gypsy put in his mouth.

"Here, Gyp," Billy lit his lighter with his left hand and held the flame towards the old man.

On the walk over, Billy didn't know how he wanted to kill Gypsy. He knew it would be done and it would be fucking brutal. It had to be done. Billy needed it. The urge and the burn wouldn't subside.

It was going to be a game-time decision and now was the time.

Billy swung with every ounce of strength. The metal knuckles made his fist a deadly weapon. In the dim light of the garage, Gypsy didn't see it coming. The knuckles impacted the old man's face just under his left eye. His bones shattered, caving his face in. Gypsy fell to the ground, trying to put his hands up.

Billy fell on him like a predator. He punched and punched, the metal knuckles smashing whatever they encountered. Whether it was Gypsy's fingers, as he reached up to block the attack, or his wide nose, which became a mangled mess. Billy rained blows, each sounding wetter and wetter. The bone splintered, pieces of it cutting his hand as he punched. It was a feeling of joy. He stopped punching, blood covering him. He breathed deeply, his lungs burning from exertion. The smell of blood mixed with shit. Gypsy must've had one final movement. Billy breathed it in like the finest perfumes. Strangely, he realized his dick was hard.

He stood looking at the unrecognizable man. Blood bubbled from his crooked mouth. Billy was pretty sure he was dead and if he wasn't, he would be soon. He didn't feel like leaving it to chance. Billy plunged the knife into Gypsy's gut, just above his pubic line. The blade slid off his pelvis and bit deep into his gut. Billy cut up, towards the old man's face. His belly opened, a purple and blue tangle of intestines severed with the slice. Billy kept cutting, forcing his knife through the rib cage. Each bone gave a pleasing audible click. He wanted to admire his handy work, but he knew sticking around was a bad idea.

Billy put the knife in his pants and walked out the door. He pulled his hood up and ran. The rain was still coming down and no one was out. Even if someone saw him, he'd just be another person trying to get out of the rain.

Billy burst into his apartment and ran to the bathroom. His cock sprung from his pants as he pulled them down. The bloody knife clattered on the floor. He started dry stroking himself. Something was missing. He bent down, picked up the knife and sliced his palm. Dream Jeff said blood was great lube. Billy knew he wasn't lying. Within seconds Billy shot a load on the bottom of the toilet seat, drops of blood leaking into the toilet. His knees were weak and he collapsed on the cold tile floor. The blood was slowing from his cut hand and his cock was a mess. The coolness of the floor relaxed him. It was dry and cool. Just before he fell asleep a thought came to the front of his mind, *It's powder dry and cool.* He slept without dreams.

CHAPTER 6

Jeannie woke up just after 10 AM. Both her throat and anus were inflamed and swollen. Her broken tooth, from Billy's final beating, still throbbed, but it was almost an afterthought. She lay there, taking a mental inventory of her ailments. The injuries were bad and she was sore, but the creeping monster of detox was her first dilemma. Slowly, she rolled over, looking around. Her rig wasn't around. Panic set in, until she realized it was in the bathroom. The last thing they wanted in the porno were drugs. Wholesome folks.

Jeannie, still naked and leaking semen out of her ass and pussy, stood. On shaky legs she walked into the bathroom. She took a long piss and after a few hard and audible pushes, she got most of the leftover spunk out of her. She grabbed her rig and went back to the bed. The heroin was mixed and within moments, she was in narcotic bliss. Until the knock on the door.

She turned her head, as if in a dream.

"Who is it?" Stupid question. I was either Deet or Rex. She hoped they had her dope. Her last bag was swimming through her veins. Realizing she was still nude, she grabbed a pair of sweatpants and t-shirt.

"It's Deet. Let me in, it's freezing."

Jeannie put her hair, which had a crunchy streak in it, in a ponytail. She really needed to wash and brush it.

"Hold on," she said, getting off the bed. She undid the chain and threw the bolt.

Deet walked in, a blustery gust following him.

Jeannie put her arms defensively across her chest; she could feel her nipples stiffen.

The big man walked in and pulled something out of his pocket. He tossed it on the bed; it was her payment. Well, it was half of her payment.

Jeannie picked up the bundle, the one single bundle and stared at it.

"Rex said 2 bunds," she stared at it as if it would magically multiply. She grabbed the money, "And $100. This is only half." She began to cry. "Deet, this is only half," she told him again, as if he didn't know.

He didn't say anything, just shrugged his massive shoulders.

Jeannie pressed the heels of her hands into her eyes. She saw stars from the pressure.

"He wants you on Ann Street in an hour, so get cleaned up," Deet said to her.

She pulled her hands away, tear streaked mascara running down her face. She didn't speak or nod.

Deet stepped up to her. "Did you hear me?" He said.

Jeannie, fearing a beating, nodded and squeaked out, "Yes."

"Good," he said, turning towards the door. "Oh, and dress warm." He left, slamming the door behind him.

An hour later, she was showered, dressed and on the street. She sucked her first dick of the day ten minutes later. She was thankful the heat was turned up in the car.

❋ ❋ ❋

Twenty minutes after Jeannie felt the reservoir tip of the condom fill with cum, Billy woke up. If he looked down the block, he would've seen the car that had picked her up, his former girlfriend stuffing a greasy handful of cash into her padded bra.

Billy realized he was on the bathroom floor. He was naked and freezing. This wasn't anything new to him, as all drunks had fallen asleep praying to the porcelain god. The only thing that struck him as odd was he wasn't hung over. He felt decent, except for his hand, which throbbed in sickening pulses. He looked down at his dick.

It was flaky brown and stuck in his pubic hair. For a second he thought he pounded Jeannie's ass again, but then he remembered she was gone.

"Gypsy," he croaked. "A nip for the fucking Gyp." The night's activities came back to him in a wave of anguish and pleasure. He'd savagely murdered an innocent, old man. It was something that repulsed and pleasured him at the same time.

"What the fuck?" Billy said to himself. He knew. The entire time, he knew. Something about the tattoo was fucking with him.

He stood, painfully peeling his dick out of his pubes and pissed.

Billy showered, the water a murky brown. He wrapped his hand in an old t-shirt, using the tape he used on his toe to keep it in place.

He went into the living area and dropped heavily on the futon. He lit up a cigarette and looked at the ceiling. Even though he'd just woken up, he felt exhausted. *Probably from sleeping on the floor*, he thought, adjusting his sore back against the relative softness of the futon. He took a final drag and put the cigarette into the ashtray, which had accumulated quite a few butts. Billy drifted off to sleep and unlike last time, he dreamt.

The dream was a good one, at least that's how it started. Billy, who was 14 again, sat on the back patio of his childhood house. He had a gnarled joint in his mouth. Steve, his buddy from down the street, sat in a chair next to him.

"Just breathe in like it's air," said Steve, handing Billy the lighter.

Billy shrugged and lit the joint. He'd smoked a cigarette once, so he knew what he was doing. Billy puffed hard, the smoke going into his lungs. He broke into an eye watering cough.

Steve started laughing, reaching for the joint. "Hell yeah," he said, taking the joint, trying to not burn himself. "I told you this was the good shit." He took his puff, coughing in turn.

"What the fuck are you doing?" yelled a voice from behind them.

Both boys, red faced, turned to see Jim Silver, Billy's dad, standing behind them.

Billy looked at Steve, but the boy was gone. Only a cloud of smoke was left. His father's strong hands were on him, yanking him from the patio chair.

Jim pushed his son into the kitchen.

"Stand there," his father told him. "April," he yelled for Billy's mother. In the real life event, Billy's mother wasn't home. In his dream state, he knew this was going to be different than the real deal.

Billy felt the house shudder as all 300 pounds of his mother came trundling down the stairs.

"What's the matter?" She said, out of breath. She leaned her bulk against the counter.

"This," said his father, holding up a smoldering joint the size of a paper towel tube.

Billy had to use every fiber in his being to fight the urge to laugh. The joint was comical to say the least.

Billy's mother gasped, putting her hands against her fat face.

"Is that--," she cut off.

"Yup," said his father. "Grass."

She burst into tears, as if she were just given a death sentence.

"How could you, Billy? Not the grass." She wailed.

"Oh, come come," a voice said from the other room. In walked Talia, wearing a white, men's dress shirt and skirt. She looked like the naughty school girls from all of the pornos Billy had seen.

Billy stared at her and in his pubescent mind, realized she wasn't wearing a bra. Her deliciously pink, pierced nipples were shadows under the shirt.

"There, there," she said, cradling Billy's mother. She rested the large woman's head on her chest. "Is that better?" she asked.

"Almost," his mother said, undoing the top button on Talia's shirt. "Almost," her fat hand, which had slid into many potato chip bags, slid into Talia's shirt. She cupped her left breast, pinching the nipple. She grabbed the barbell piercing, tugging it ever so slightly. Talia cooed. "That's a little better."

"Well, I think I can help," said Talia, ripping the shirt off.

Billy's mother descended on her breasts, sucking on them, her chins wobbling as she moved from left to right. She bit on the piercings, looking Talia in the eyes as she pulled on them.

"Give me that cunt," his mother growled.

Talia obliged, hopping up on the counter. Her skirt pulled up past her belly button. Billy, in his stupor, watched her clean shaven vagina spread, the moisture keeping her lips closed for just a second longer. Ravenously, his mother descended on her, lapping her like a dog.

"Now, young man, what are we going to do about this?" Billy's father said, the stinky joint in his face.

Billy, disgusted, yet clearly aroused, watched the performance.

Talia had her fingers in the other woman's hair, but her eyes were locked on Billy's.

Billy's father slapped him in the face. "Hey, I'm fucking talking to you!" The big man stood red faced and nose to nose with him.

"I ah--" stammered Billy.

"My turn," Talia said and in an instant, his mother was nude.

"Oh, God," Billy muttered.

Billy's mother, her face slick with Talia's pussy juice, kissed the other woman. Her floppy, massive breasts sat on her stomach. Her stomach hung down, covering her cunt, but Billy could still see a thick, black patch of hair sticking out of the folds.

In a feat of strength only seen in dreams, Talia picked the woman up and sat her on the counter. Her face disappeared in the muff, as Billy's mother moaned in a way he could've gone his entire life without hearing.

Talia pulled her face from his mother's crotch and looked at him. Instead of pussy juice, she was covered in blood. She grinned. Her mouth was full of sharp, yellow teeth. She bit his mother in the thigh, bloody teeth marks oozed.

"Oh, fuck yes!" his mother moaned, in ecstasy. "Fucking eat me!"

Talia took another bite, this time in the stomach. The next one, she took off the fat woman's left nipple.

Billy's mother was sweating, eyes closed, pulling at her hair. It came off with bloody clumps of scalp.

He knew where the next bite was going, but he couldn't look away.

Talia ripped into his mother's throat. Blood oozed around her suckling mouth.

"Hey, save some for me," came a slurred voice

from behind.

Billy turned as the newcomer entered the house.

"You got a nip for the Gyp?" Gypsy asked. His face was a bloody mess of bone and brain matter. His jaw hung loose, making his words almost undecipherable.

Billy turned back to the performance and was again nose to nose with his father.

His father grinned and punched him in the stomach.

Billy looked down and saw the knuckle knife sticking out of his gut. With a powerful pull, his father slid the blade up to his ribs. Sliced intestinal and stomach matter landed on Billy's feet. He collapsed, but wasn't granted an end to this nightmare yet.

Talia had eaten his mother's throat down to the spine. She lay there, her head lolled back and dead. The look of pleasure rested on her face.

"You know, Billy," said his father, who unzipped his fly, "I've heard blood is the best lube."

Talia spit blood on his grotesquely large cock. She gave it a loving stroke and bent over the counter, placing both hands on Billy's mother's corpse to steady herself.

The last image in his mind, just before the nightmare ended, was his father thrusting away, Talia's pussy spreading with each bloody plunge. She looked back, growling through yellow teeth.

Billy woke up in a panic. The growling was next to his head.

Instinctively Billy put his hands in front of his face, just as the beast attacked. But it didn't attack, because it wasn't there.

It was the middle of the night, but the streetlights provided enough light to see. Billy couldn't see anything. He grabbed his cell phone and turned on the flashlight. The small bulb didn't put out much light, but it was enough for him to find his way to the light switch. Before flipping it on, Billy grabbed his knife. The knuckles were still grimy with blood. He was prepared for an attack when the light came on. Nothing came. He searched the room, but only found one old needle and a bunch of dust bunnies.

Billy's heart began to calm, as he lay back down. He left the knife in bed next to him and slept.

❊ ❊ ❊

Billy spent most of the next day watching TV and thinking. The only time he left was to buy a pack of cigarettes, which he was quickly going through.

A heavy, cold rain fell on the city. Gray water ran through the streets. Boats of trash ripped along the sidewalks. Most of it hung up in the sewer drains, but some made it.

Traffic, especially pedestrian traffic, was light. Cars still zipped around the city. The yellow taxis, which were cars of every make and model, drove without care. Tidal waves sprung up where they passed. They blared their horns to let their fares know they'd arrived. God forbid if they got out.

Billy watched the rat race below. He sat at the window, cigarette in hand. The cool air sucked the smoke out into the world. He took a drag and flicked it out of the window.

It had been almost 24 hours since he'd killed Gypsy. He rode the high of that kill for most of the day, which let him rest, but it was wearing off. Just to keep his urge in check, he'd gnawed the stump of his finger raw. Blood dribbled from it. That wasn't going to be enough. The tattoo was getting hot and knew something was going to have to happen.

Something he hadn't heard in a while drew his attention; his phone. Billy grabbed it from the futon and saw he had a notice from *The Lucky Draw*. He saw the title of the email.

"The return of *Shit Fist*," he read aloud. He opened the email, anger rising in him.

Hey, everyone. The members of Shit Fist want to offer a formal apology for our last show. The conduct of our FORMER lead singer and guitar player, Billy Silver, is not what we're about. We love our music and what it represents, but most of all we love our fans. We are happy to introduce our new lead singer, Aaron Dollenger. Aaron is an Ohio native, who recently moved to the area. He has a scream like no other and fits perfectly with the band. In a show of good faith in music, we're playing this Saturday night and to keep prices lower, not taking any money for it. Please come out and support your local bands. Doors at 7, show at 9. Thank you all.

Dillon Peck

Billy read over and over, each time getting more and more pissed off. He threw his phone across the room.

"Fucking cock sucking motherfuckers!" He yelled. In one swipe, he threw all the garbage from his table. "Cunt, shit eater, fucks! Some fucking faggot thinks he's playing my music, singing my songs! Not a fucking chance!" When he looked at his phone, initially he realized it was Friday night. "Alright, tomorrow, motherfuckers. We'll see." Billy pulled his long hair. It hurt, but felt good. The rage was subsiding as the burn of the tattoo grew in intensity. "Fuck!" he screamed. He needed to end this. The tattoo was killing him. He needed fucking answers and he needed them now.

Billy put his shoes on and grabbed his jacket. He was going to get his answers.

❋ ❋ ❋

Billy was soaked to the bone, but the tattoo shop was just around the corner. He stopped before turning the corner; a kamikaze taxi was coming and he didn't want to get blasted. *Fucker probably wouldn't even stop.* The taxi blew by, blasting a tidal wave of filth.

Billy trotted around the corner and stopped. He looked up at the street sign. It was the right fucking street, but something was wrong.

He went over to the boarded-up storefront. The plywood was covered in graffiti and fliers. Many were unreadable from the weather, but he found one that was legible.

"What the fuck?" he whispered. The flier was over a year old. Billy banged on the door, which was completely covered. "Hello!" he yelled, kicking the door. "Open the fuck up!" He pulled the handle to no avail. Next, he moved to the boarded-up windows, trying to pry them off.

This can't be it. It must be farther down, he thought. He could have all the good thoughts in the world, it wasn't going to make it appear.

Rage, confusion and fear swept over him. The rain picked up. He was getting nowhere with the shop. He was going to walk around the block, but he knew it was pointless. This was his to deal with and no one else's.

It was nearly dark and with thick clouds overhead, visibility was next to nothing. Billy started home. The tattoo burned and a wave of dread washed over him. It felt like he was in the principal's office all over again and they were waiting for his parents to get there. He knew he was in trouble, but didn't know how much.

A young woman popped out of one of the buildings. She had a blue raincoat on and heavy boots. As she turned her head, Billy could see she had white headphones over her ears.

This was his only chance. It was risky, but at this juncture, he didn't give a fuck.

Another cab came blasting down the street and Billy acted.

He ran up behind the girl, her music allowing him to do so without being heard.

"What the fuck?" was the last thing she said, as Billy threw her in front of the cab.

Billy didn't stop to watch his handy work. If he had, he would've seen her get sucked underneath the car. Her head stuck in between the front axle, decapitating her. The rest of her body ended up tangled, bloody mess, wrapped around the back tires.

The cab dragged her body, the rain making his car slide. A trail of blood ran down the street, where one of her heavy boots still lay.

Billy didn't even break his stride. He had a plan. He was determined. He had a date with a knife.

❈ ❈ ❈

Billy fingered the blade of the knife. Gypsy's bones had dulled it slightly, but it was still sharp. He hoped so. He turned on the hot plate and took a seat at the table. For the first time in a while, he wished he had a little bit of dope. If only to just dull the pain of what he was about to do.

Billy wore a wife beater tank top, which was once white. He stared at the tattoo. The face in one section of it stared back at him. He didn't know what she did, but if he ever saw Talia again, he was going to fucking kill her. He might consider raping her first, but she looked pretty fit and might put up a fight. There was always the option of fucking her after he killed her. She wouldn't mind.

He could think about killing and corpse rape later. Now, he had a job to do and it was going to be less than pleasant.

The knife bit into his flesh with ease. He felt it get through the first couple layers of skin. He hoped it was far enough. Blood dripped down his arm, ran over the tattoo. He sliced down, peeling his skin off. The pain was brutal. He sliced along side and underneath the tattoo, making a bloody frame around it. Billy reached down with his mouth and took the flap of skin in his teeth. He began to tear, ripping the skin off his arm like a sheet from a filthy bed. It became snagged, so he went at it with the knife. Blood ran freely down his arm, but he didn't give a fuck. The tattoo was coming off. When Billy saw bare muscle, he realized he'd cut too far. Oh well, he was already going. His mouth was red with his own blood. He bit down on the flesh tag and ripped. His screams were stifled by the skin, but he growled in pain...and pleasure.

Billy never heard flesh rip, but it sounded like fabric. An odd thought as he tore a piece of himself off. The blood poured from him. He definitely cut too deep. The room was getting fuzzy on his periphery. With one final pull, the chunk of skin, tattoo and all, came off. Billy spat it on the ground.

Blood dripped from his fingertips as he stood on uneasy legs. He stumbled to the counter and grabbed the hotplate. Without a second thought, he jammed it onto the open wound. Billy shuddered with pain, held it as long as possible and passed out.

CHAPTER 7

Jeannie's head hurt. It wasn't a headache, but a lump on her forehead.

The previous night, one of her johns decided he wanted to take her from behind. Rather than do it in his car, he decided to go into an alley. In his excitement, he thrust just a little too hard, smacking her head off the brick wall. She cried out and stumbled for a second, but that didn't stop him. Without ceremony, he ripped the cum filled condom off and threw it in the alley. He'd already paid (T-Rex's rule) and was in his car before she could even pull her skirt back down. She wasn't bleeding, but she could feel the skin had been rubbed raw in the spot and a bump was already rising.

She rolled out of bed and went into the bathroom. She did something she tried to avoid; she looked in the mirror.

Jeannie's hair was stringy and unkempt. She

would brush it when she remembered, but it was just so unhealthy, it didn't matter. Her face wasn't much better. The acne was back. Her hollow cheeks were ripe with it. When she went out to work, she would cake on makeup in hopes of covering it. Not that the johns really cared about a little acne, but that wasn't the point. Her eyes were sunken and black-rimmed and her broken tooth was starting to show the first signs of rot. She'd lost weight too. When she was in high school, she had an amazing body. High and firm breasts, a toned midsection and an ass you could bounce quarters off of. Now, her breasts had lost any youth she'd tried to save. They sagged, which wasn't an issue, gravity happened. They were veiny and her nipples looked puckered. Her stomach looked like she'd had 12 kids. A wrinkly pooch hung just enough to notice and her ass defied the odds, being both flat and pot marked with cellulite.

Jeannie grabbed her rig. She only had 2 bags left from the bundle Rex had given her. She didn't even know how long ago that was. Time was a blur. It was get up, shoot up, fuck, suck, repeat. Sometimes not in that order.

Someone knocked on her door.

She knew it was Deet. Rex would rarely

knock. He would use the key that he'd taken and let himself in more often than not.

She left the dope on the counter and walked to the door.

"Hey, Deet," she said letting the big man in the room.

He grimaced at the conditions she was living in. Fast food wrappers, Chinese take-out containers and used condoms decorated the window sill and night stands.

"Rex wanted me to stop by and check on you," he said, looking at the bump on her head.

She stared at him, wondering what he was looking at, then she remembered. "Oh, this?" She touched the bump. "It's nothing. I'm still good to go." Jeannie knew the 2 bags would barely get her through the rest of the day, let alone tomorrow.

Deet grabbed her chin, not hard, but not gently either, and examined her face.

"Who did it?" he said in an almost protective way.

Jeannie was touched, but only for a second. He wasn't protecting his girlfriend or sister, no, they were protecting their business venture.

"Deet, really it was an accident. He was a regular who just gave a hard thrust when he nutted. He even apologized and offered to get me some ice," she lied.

He looked skeptical, but didn't push the issue. "Clean up and hit the streets," he said. "Rex said there may be a bonus for you. Apparently your video is doing pretty well and he's getting another offer for a repeat performance. I'll let you get ready." He walked out, leaving her there alone.

Jeannie walked back to the bathroom and prepped her dope. She sat on the bed, trying to steady her hand. She cried, her body shook. How had she fallen so far from the girl who was a track star, B student, with a steady boyfriend, to a heroin addicted prostitute? She wasn't an angel, but after high school everything was going ok for her. Community college was going well, and she had a decent job. The day her life took a shit was the day she met Billy Silver. She'd never been punched by a man before him. Hell, she was a virgin until she was 18. Now she was getting gang banged for heroin.

Snot ran down her face, but she didn't care. Like the professional she was, she timed her injection between sobs. The heroin flooded into her, dulling her fried senses, numbing everything.

❋ ❋ ❋

Billy's arm burned, but in the best way possible. It was the painful, pusy, second degree burn that Billy was feeling, not the burning urge to hurt himself or others.

After cutting the tattoo off and cauterizing the wound, Billy had slept like a baby. His body was physically and emotionally exhausted.

Billy took to his new favorite place, sitting by the window, and smoked a cigarette. He had to use his left hand to hold it. The stub of his severed finger was almost healed, but the missing bit made holding the cigarette odd. Normally he'd be using his right hand, but the massive, bloody blister on his arm protested in agony. Even moving his hand caused waves of pain.

Billy looked at his handy work in a mixture of fear and awe. The raw patch of flesh was buttery yellow and bubbled. Blood still oozed from the edges of the blisters. His arm was tacky with old blood and puss from already popped blisters.

He put the cigarette out and pulled out his phone. The notice from Dillon was burned into his mind. He read it over and over. The band was his baby. The one thing in his life he was good at and loved.

Billy was no saint, but his life took a definite turn for the worse when that cunt Jeannie came into his life. She knew just how to piss him off and get under his skin. Anything she could do to piss him off, she did. Billy always had a bit of a temper, but she brought out the worst in him. The first few times he put his hands on her, he felt guilty afterwards. Now, he didn't give a fuck. She deserved every punch, slap and surprise anal.

Billy's calm demeanor faded as his anger at his former lover grew.

He put a hand on his chest. A bout of heartburn was on the horizon. The subtle burning crept up. He didn't think he had any antacids, but he'd check.

Billy stood, the burning got worse. He stopped, panic ripping through him. In three strides he was in the bathroom in front of the mirror. He ripped his shirt off, his burned arm screaming in pain.

Billy wasn't one to cry, in fact he only did a few times as an adult. As he stared at the tattoo, which was perfectly inked over his heart, he knew this would be one of those times.

* * *

It was dark. Billy didn't know what time it was, but he knew it was dark outside. He sat at the table. The ashtray forest of butts was full again, but he didn't give a fuck. After tonight nothing mattered.

He was a dead man and he knew it. The tattoo and that fucking bitch, Talia signed his death warrant. Well, Billy Silver was no pussy. He'd go out on his own terms and by God, he'd take some motherfuckers with him.

He looked at his phone. It was just before 8 PM. He still had time.

The final pieces of his plan were falling into place. He didn't care either way. Tonight would be the final ballad of Billy Silver.

He flicked a lamp on and dug under the futon. He grabbed an old bookbag, but kept searching until he found what he was looking for. A grin split his face as he threw the item in the bag. *This will help*, he thought.

Billy put a hoodie on, threw the bag over his shoulder and slid the knife into his waistband. Just before he walked out, he froze. He turned around and ripped the utensil drawer out. Using the light of his cell phone, he found what he was looking for. The corkscrew must've been left by the previous tenants, because Billy never had a use for it. Well, he had a use for it now. He pocketed it and walked out into the night.

❋ ❋ ❋

Jeannie was tired. Luckily, tonight had been mainly a blowjob night, so she was able to keep her clothes on and stay in cars. She opened her mouth wide, stretching her jaw. It creaked, but she had worse.

She took off her 'work uniform', a leopard print jacket, button up shirt, push up bra, and skirt. Most of her johns wanted to get sucked off, so she started wearing tights to help her stay warm. If any of them actually wanted to fuck, they were easy enough to pull down. Most guys just wanted to pump away and bust, so even if she fucked outside it wasn't that long of an ordeal.

Jeannie put on a sweatshirt and pajama pants and evaluated her stash. She was out of dope. Deet said he'd be up to pay her. She knew what that meant; she'd have to blow him before getting her money and drugs.

On cue, there was a knock on the door.

"It's open," she said, sitting on the edge of the bed. She was already putting her hair in a ponytail.

Deet walked in, closing the door behind him. He stood in front of her. He looked down and smiled.

Without having to ask or even say a word, she unzipped his fly. She took her shirt off, exposing her bare breasts.

"Can you nut on my tits tonight? I really don't want to wash my hair," she said, stroking his semi-hard cock.

Deet grinned at her. "I got you, girl. You just do your thing."

Jeannie did. She did it well and in a few minutes she was wiping cum off her chest with tissues.

Deet put his cock back in his pants and reached in his pocket. He gave her a bundle of dope and a handful of cash.

"Here," he said, handing it to her as she put

her shirt back on. "Rex said you got another movie in a few days." He looked her over. "Maybe get a cheeseburger or two. Your skinny ass is looking like bones." Deet walked out.

Jeannie wanted to shoot up, but she needed a shower before anything. If she shot up first, she'd probably pass out.

She undressed and walked into the bathroom. She put the water as hot as she could stand it. Her skin turned red. Then, she turned it up just a little more.

❋ ❋ ❋

Billy was a hunter and he'd found his prey. For years he'd been under their grasp, whether it was one dealer or another. Not anymore. Tonight, that changed.

T-Rex, Deet and a couple more of their 'boys' stood on the corner.

It was dark, but Billy knew it was them. The light of the bodega was more than enough to identify them.

"Yo, Rex," Billy said, stepping out of the shadows. He raised a hand as the drug dealer looked around for who called his name.

"Eh, Rex, who the fuck is that?" said one of his friends.

Rex looked at him. "Some fucking junkie," he paused. "One that fucking owes me money." He started walking towards Billy. His friends started to follow. "Na, we good. If I can't handle a fucking junkie, kill my ass." He turned back to Billy. "You got my fucking money?" He said, still walking towards Billy.

Billy had his hands in his hoodie pocket. He was hunched over, posed as a victim.

"Yeah, I have it for you."

T-Rex smiled, still getting closer. "Good. Your girl tried to pay your debt with her ass, but you still fucking owe me. That bitch is a useless hoe." He stepped closer, right in Billy's face. "Gim'ee my money," he said.

"Ok," said Billy, pulling his hand out of his hoodie. Instead of cash, he held his knife. He thrust all 6 inches of cheap, Chinese steel into T-Rex's belly.

The drug dealer gasped, looking down at the knuckle knife sticking out of his gut.

Billy pulled the blade out, the metal wet with blood.

Rex was having trouble breathing and unknown to him, Billy had sliced the bottom of his right lung. The lung collapsed and blood bubbled from his mouth. He collapsed into Billy's arms. His lips moved like a fish out of water, but no sound came out.

"Hey, Deet!" Billy yelled, lowering the dying drug dealer to the ground. "Rex collapsed," he said, waving the big man over. Billy could feel the warmth of blood on him. He hoped the darkness would keep Deet from seeing it.

Deet hustled over, the other guys watching, but not walking.

They may have been hanging with Rex, but it didn't mean they were best of friends.

Billy was panting, the look of panic in his eyes. "I don't fucking know what happened," Billy said as Deet got closer. "He just fell into my arms." Deet crouched down.

Billy struck, fast and accurate. The first 4 inches of the blade pierced Deet's skull with a smack.

The big man died instantly, pulling Billy to the ground, the knife still stuck in his head.

Billy yanked, but it was jammed. Thick bone held tight, gripping the blade.

The other guys on the corner approached, but none too fast. They didn't seem to really care about the assault. Actually, they had cell phone cameras out, recording the whole thing.

"Yo, this crazy little nigga just dropped his ass," one said, the light from his camera bobbing with excitement. They didn't get too close, just in case Billy turned his rage on them.

"I got them sneaks," one of them said.

"Nah, nigga, they's mine." Another responded.

"Fuck you, they match my Gucci belt," the first said.

For a second Billy thought they were going to try and steal his shoes, then he realized it was Rex's shoes they were talking about. He relaxed, knowing they didn't have retaliation on their minds. There was one more thing he needed and he'd be on his way. Billy wrenched the knife, but it was still stuck. He twisted and the cheap steel snapped with a 'ting' sound. The handle had just under 3 inches of the blade left, but luckily for Billy, it came to a fine point. It was more like a needle than a knife.

Billy sat on Rex's chest, making more blood

bubble up from his mouth. He placed the point under the man's eye.

"Where the fuck in Jeannie?" Billy asked, adding pressure to the blade.

Rex was turning blue. He let out a weak cry, trying to speak.

"Imp-Imperial," he croaked, the knife causing a little blood spot on his eye. "408," he mumbled. He reached into his pocket.

Billy pushed the knife deeper, puncturing the eye.

Rex thrashed, causing his pierced lung to spit more blood.

"Key," he moaned in agony. Rex pulled a key on a tag from his pocket. Room 408.

"Thanks," Billy said, leaning his entire body weight on the handle of the knife. Rex bucked and kicked, but the blade popped his eyeball and entered his brain before he could muster anymore of a fight. The rest of the blade snapped off, but Billy was done with it. He had something else for Jeannie.

He walked away and before he was around the corner, the crowd descended on the two corpses, kindly removing all their personal belongings.

* * *

Jeannie felt refreshed. There was nothing like a hot shower and cleanish clothes. She sat on the edge of the bed, the needle already loaded with heroin and ready to go. She hummed "This Little Piggy" this time deciding between her little toe.

The needle went in and her flesh wrapped lovingly around it. Jeannie, for the last time ever, pushed the plunger down.

That felt like a hot bag, she thought, slipping into slumber, which would soon lead to death's sweet embrace.

* * *

Billy opened the door to 408 and saw Jeannie lying facedown on the bed. She didn't move, but she was breathing. Barely breathing.

"Wake up, you fucking bitch!" he yelled, the corkscrew in his right hand. The burn on his arm pulsed, but he didn't care. He was on a mission. Billy kicked her in the leg. She didn't move. He stared at her as she took her final breath. "No, no fucking way you're going to deny me this! This, this is all your fault," he spat. "No, you're going to pay." He ripped her pants off. He had no desire to fuck her and what he did next wasn't the least bit sexual.

With a little effort, Billy jammed the corkscrew up her ass.

Jeannie didn't even flinch. She was gone.

Billy shoved it as far as it would go, blood and shit leaked out. He twisted and twisted until metal bit into flesh. He grinned, twisting more, careful not to tear her rectum. Billy pulled. Nothing happened at first and then her body let go.

Jeannie's large intestine came slithering out like a giant earthworm.

Billy pulled and pulled, until the entire 5 feet of the large intestine was on the floor. Next came the smaller coils of her small intestine. Billy kept pulling, but eventually tangled himself in the gut. He reached for his knife to cut free, forgetting he left it back with the dealers. Like a man possessed, Billy grabbed a chunk of intestine and bit into it. Blood and half digested shit, flooded into his mouth. He ripped and teared until he was free. He didn't care, he just needed to get out. He had one more stop to make.

The tattoo now on his chest was burning. It craved death and carnage and Billy was going to give it what it wanted.

* * *

"Check, check," Aaron said into the microphone. "Sound guy," he said, looking at the guy in the loft with the soundboard. "How am I?" He asked.

The sound guy, whose name was Ryan Ciric, and wouldn't survive the night, gave a thumbs up.

Aaron adjusted his earpiece, hearing the rest of his band mates tuning their instruments. They all gave him a thumbs up. He looked into the crowd. He was blinded by the hot overhead lights, but he could make out some faces here and there.

"What's up, you motherfuckers!" he yelled into the mic. The crowd returned the screams with vigor. "We are, *Shit Fist*," he growled, pulling the mic from the stand.

Dillon tapped his sticks.

Their set was underway.

* * *

Billy watched the entrance of *The Lucky Draw* from the corner. The sound of music leaked from the brick walls.

Billy watched Maurice, the massive bouncer, sit at the front door.

Maurice was an imposing force, who'd thrown quite a few people a great distance, but he had a weakness. His bladder was the size of an 8 year old's and he loved his energy drinks.

Maurice upended a big can of some new drink and set it down.

Billy just had to wait.

His chance came 5 minutes later.

Maurice walked around the side of the building, leaving the front door unguarded.

Billy pulled the straps on his bookbag tight and jogged towards the door. His bag was heavier than when he left home, but it would be lighter in a few minutes.

He walked into *The Lucky Draw*. It was fairly

dark, the main lighting shone on the band up on stage. His fucking band.

Some fucking asshole belted out *his* lyrics and the fans were actually cheering. Billy saw a pretty decent mosh pit in front of the stage. A bigger one than he was ever able to conjure.

The room was packed with bodies and stunk like it too. He noticed a different bartender. Jeff probably got fired for the little cock grabbing escapade.

Billy set his backpack down and reached inside. He pulled the bike lock out and wrapped it around the two door handles. No one noticed, they were focused on the band, who started into their next song.

He walked into the crowd, almost to the front row. A few people gave him dirty looks, but he didn't care. He was on the edge of the mosh pit, when he grabbed the gas cans out of his bookbag. The first one, he upended on himself. It was strangely cold. Well, that would certainly change in the next few moments. The other 2 were smaller and instead of spouts, they had rags stuffed in them.

People moved away from him, but the room was so packed, there wasn't anywhere to go.

Billy pulled his lighter from his pocket.

People were screaming now. Not screams of joy and love of music, no they were screams of sheer terror.

With one turn of the wheel, Billy lit the lighter. His gasoline-soaked body immolated in a fiery breath. He grabbed the other two gas cans, his flaming hands lit them instantly. Before his muscles and nerves were beyond function, he threw them. The first onto the stage.

The flaming can hit the singer in the chest, burping fire into his face. He turned in panic, kicking the can. Sammy and Vin tried to move, but little fireballs caught their pants. They ran, spreading the flames to the old stage curtains.

The second can, Billy hurled at the back door; the only other exit from the inferno. It hit the wall and a pool of fire flowed towards the horrified crowd. Tendrils of flame snaked up the wall.

Billy watched the chaos, the flames crawling over him almost an afterthought.

People were trampled underfoot, their screams drowned out by hundreds of others. The oxygen was burned from the air as more and more people caught on fire. Bodies crushed against the front door, which was chained shut.

The power went out. The only light was fire. Human infernos ran frantically, like embers floating above a campfire. Within that fire he saw Talia, a hot grin across her face.

Before his eyeballs melted and everything went black, Billy thought of Mrs. Lamberg's High School English class. In the 11th grade, she made them all read Ray Bradbury's classic novel, *Fahrenheit 451*, and its classic opening line stuck with him.

Billy's melted eyes ran down his face. His throat was scorched and raw flesh. His lungs collapsed and his blood was on the verge of boiling.

That opening line was the last thing he thought before he went to black.

"It was a pleasure to burn." Yes, yes it was.

EPILOGUE

Hector adjusted the bookbag just enough to get to the hood of his jacket. It was cold and he needed to get home. He was sure the kittens were cold too. Well, they were tucked nice and cozy in the bookbag. They were barely 3 days old, so they didn't know what cold even was. They were just concerned about getting a tit. Hell, their eyes were still closed. They wiggled and mewled as he adjusted again.

He turned the corner and stopped. A new tattoo shop opened up, but that wasn't what caught his attention. The first thing that stopped him on this blustery day was the smoking hot woman behind the windows. The second thing, and his reason for entering the shop was the sign advertising money for a tattoo.

Hector walked in. It smelled clean, like antiseptic. So far so good. The artwork on the walls was interesting, not quite his style, but not bad. He didn't really care about the art, he was more concerned about the artist.

"Can I help you?" the woman behind the counter said. She wore a perfectly tight, ¾ sleeve black sweater. Her full breasts were barely contained in the shirt. She had pale, white skin, with black hair. She wore it down, which Hector loved.

Hector got lost in her oil slick eyes and had to remember why he was there.

"Ah, yeah. I was wondering about the paid tat. I'm looking for some new ink. You know, something new and fresh in my life," he licked his lips in as seductive of a way as he could.

"Oh, great," she said. "I'm Talia," she extended her hand.

Hector shook it. It was powder dry and cool. "Hector. Nice to meet you."

She seemed to look him over, holding his hand for just a moment longer than socially acceptable.

"I was looking for someone with big, thick," she let it hang in the air for just a second, "arms, to tattoo." She blushed and swept her hair behind her left ear.

Hector leaned on the counter between them. It was time to turn on the Spanish charm.

"Well, mommy, my arms aren't the only big, thick things around here." He gave her a smirk. He knew that was a lie. As a matter of fact, he was embarrassed about how small his cock was. A prostitute actually laughed at him before. He knocked her teeth out in the alley behind a laundromat.

"I'm open right now, if you want to come in the back," she said.

Hector felt the kittens moving. He hoped they weren't pissing and shitting in the bag.

"Are you gonna be around in like an hour?" He asked, hoping she couldn't hear the kittens. "I have to run home and feed the dog."

"Sure," she said. "I'll get everything set up. In fact, I have the perfect design for you."

ABOUT THE AUTHOR

Daniel J. Volpe

Daniel J. Volpe is an author of extreme horror and splatterpunk. His love for horror started at a young age when his grandfather unwittingly rented him A Nightmare on Elm Street. Daniel has published some of his stories with Raven's Inn Press, Sirens Call publications, Twisted Tales, Exiles Literary magazine, Literati Publications and self publishing. He can be found on Facebook @ Daniel J. Volpe and Instagram @dj_volpe_author.

Made in the USA
Monee, IL
08 June 2025